1

THE SPHERE OF LIGHT

Secrets of the Boleyn women

A Novel

First published in 2023 by Doonreaghan Press, Doonreagan, Cashel, Co. Galway H91 R6Y5, Ireland.
Email: doonreaghanpress@gmail.com

ISBN for this publication is: 978-0-9539033-6-8.

Cover design by Serhii Shuklanskyi.
Castle drawing by Ebba Pate.

Printed by Swallowtail Print.

With thanks to

Elaine Montgomerie

for long-term inspiration and support

"Convincing and deeply moving, The Sphere of Light brings brand new insights into the Boleyn story."

Dr Damien Duffy.

"This captivating novel is sumptuous in detail and thrillingly plotted. A triumph."

Dr Owen Emmerson.

CONTENTS:

Foreword

Having married a descendant of Henry Carey, Lord Hunsdon, son of Mary Boleyn and, presumably, King Henry VIII of England, I have spent decades researching the history of the Boleyn family. Hunsdon, first cousin and likely half-brother of Queen Elizabeth I, rose to eminence during his lifetime. As Lord Chamberlain, he was the patron of Shakespeare's company, The Lord Chamberlain's Men. On his death, he was given an impressive memorial in Westminster Abbey.

I found myself intrigued by the still open questions surrounding this family: Why was Mary, the king's sweetheart, suddenly banished from court without an explanation? Why were Thomas and George Boleyn, favourites of the king, ignominiously stripped of their high offices in 1525, only to be gloriously reinstated a few months later? Why did the ambitious George settle for a seemingly loveless marriage of little material or social benefit? How did a purportedly lecherous king agree to spend seven years in celibacy waiting for Anne Boleyn to come to his bed? What drove him to risk so much to make Anne his wife, only to have her executed, along with George and four close associates, on trumped-up charges of adultery, incest and treason? And what induced Jane, first to give fatal evidence against her own husband and sister-in-law, and, at a later date, to encourage Queen Katheryn Howard to commit adultery, at the expense of her own head?

Added to the mysteries was the discovery of an old tombstone in the grounds of Clonony Castle in Co. Offaly, Ireland. It contradicted the commonly held view that George and

Jane Boleyn never had any offspring. One George Boleyn, who died in 1603, known as the Dean of Lichfield, has been dismissed as "some distant relation".

The Irish tombstone suggested otherwise, and the novel developed from there.

BOLEYN FAMILY TREE
(simplified)

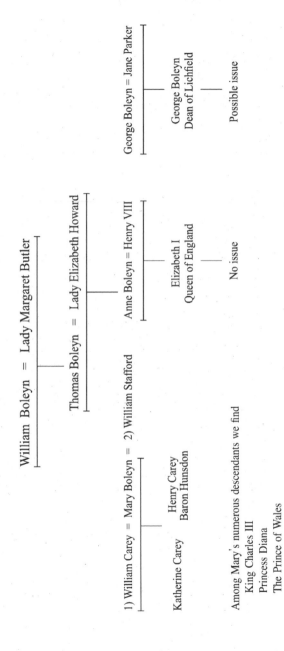

William Boleyn = Lady Margaret Butler

Thomas Boleyn = Lady Elizabeth Howard

George Boleyn = Jane Parker

George Boleyn
Dean of Lichfield

Possible issue

Anne Boleyn = Henry VIII

Elizabeth I
Queen of England

No issue

1) William Carey = Mary Boleyn = 2) William Stafford

Henry Carey
Baron Hunsdon

Katherine Carey

Among Mary's numerous descendants we find
King Charles III
Princess Diana
The Prince of Wales
Prince Harry.

13

The Sphere of Light

Goodness me — she was right! The little old woman from Yoxall. Not a witch — but a visionary! A long dark tunnel, just as she said, and at the mouth of it, a sphere of brilliant light!

The poor woman — dragged along the streets of Lichfield accused of witchcraft and heresy. Brought to me by townspeople incensed by her challenge to sacred, time-honoured beliefs: penance and expiation. Purgatory and divine retribution...

Her contention was that only the truth can save our souls, release the spirit from whatever holds it captive on earth. And if we choose to evade it in life, a second chance is granted when we die. We enter a sphere of light: a realm suspended between life and death, where your spirit is still fully sentient, even though the heart has stopped beating. And there, within that luminous orb, all knowledge, all insight, are within reach...

The townspeople wished to see her burnt at the stake.

I'm glad now that in the end I let her go.

In life, she insisted, the one thing that matters is the truth. Truth as a state of being, where doubt and misgivings are dispelled by a clear understanding of motives, causes and connections. An ideal state, she called it, to which everyone should be aspiring, though many, for reasons of their own, shy away from it.

Hm. I had my reasons to shy away. Ever since events in my early life left me with no option but to live a lie. Grow up to be a modest clergyman, in due course Dean of Lichfield. I had little to gain — and a whole lot to lose — from revealing my true identity as the only legitimate child of George Boleyn, Lord Rochford, brother of Anne Queen of England. No way could I admit to any association with my infamous Boleyn relations, convicted of the most heinous crimes.

I was helped by the fact that my origins remained unknown. My birth was never registered, and there is no record of the years I spent as a child at Hever Castle.

I never forgot the little old woman from Yoxall, the serenity of her vision. As late as yesterday – was it yesterday? I don't know, time is no longer of essence – anyway, as I drew my last breath, I found myself thinking: If only... If the little old woman in Yoxall was right... it would take the sting out of death. Turn it into something quite appealing.

And so, here I am, in the sphere of light, eons away from all worldly concerns. Is the truth really attainable here? Will the manifold mysteries lurking in my past finally be unravelled? The mere prospect is enough balm for my soul, plagued for so long by the horrific events I lived through in my childhood. Even in their day they were considered unfathomable, and I have no doubt that, to posterity, that's how they will continue to appear. But somewhere there must be an explanation, a reason why it all happened the way it did. I'm in no doubt that, buried somewhere, is a story that, like all God's creation, makes perfect sense.

Oh, for a chance of seeing some true justification, some acceptable reason, for the gruesome fate that befell my loved ones! Is it too much to hope?

If indeed it were possible, where would I start? I suppose with the one who caused me the greatest pain – the woman whose name I spent a lifetime trying to forget.

My mother. Jane Boleyn. Lady Rochford...

Good grief! No sooner has the thought crossed my mind than she appears in front of me. Looking just as I remember her: supremely elegant in court dress: a stiff kirtle of black damask, a silver-grey velvet gown, embroidered wide sleeves and a gable hood. The sumptuous clothes do little to hide the gaunt angular frame and her pinched drawn face. I've heard it said that she was once considered to be good-looking – it goes to show what spite and bitterness can do to a person's appearance.

"Mother...?" I begin tentatively.

"Don't call me that!" she snaps.

"Are you not my mother?" I ask. "Is that it?"

In reply, only silence.

"Did you not give birth to me?" I venture.

"Alas I did," is her curt answer.

Then the words come tumbling out of me, all the questions that have been plaguing me all my life, questions I never had a chance to ask her:

"Well then – why did you never love me like a mother would? What did I do to offend you?"

I can hear my voice breaking. "Mother – why did you hate me so?"

Her narrow lips grow even thinner. The look she gives me is full of loathing.

"Please answer me!" I entreat her.

Turning on her heel, she mutters: "Ask Mary."

"Mother – wait!" I cry. "I have more queries for you!"

She is gone.

So much for uncovering the truth. It seems that, even in death, my mother is determined to remain an enigma.

"Ask Mary," she said. She must have been referring to my dear aunt. Kind, gentle Mary Boleyn, who did love me, who took over a mother's role when I was rejected by my own, dangled me on her lap along with her own little ones. Mary had a heart big enough for the three of us...

And here she is! Coming towards me, smiling sweetly, her arms wide open. She is dressed more modestly, though every bit as tastefully, as her sister-in-law.

"Jojo!" she coos tenderly. "At last! I thought you'd never die!"

As so many times before, I lose myself in her soft warm embrace.

"Dearest Mary," I say. "As lovely as ever!"

At which she smiles demurely.

"Now," I add quickly, to have it over and done with, "tell me what you know about my parents."

Mary's smile evaporates. She turns away, seemingly distressed. I try to hold on to her, but she has already drawn back, into the shadows from which she came.

Oh dear. This is not going well. Perhaps the spirits of women find this kind of exploration particularly painful. I might be better off appealing to a man. Like my father...

And look, he's right in front of me! George Boleyn the Elder, Lord Rochford. Dashingly handsome, dressed to the teeth in his usual courtier's attire: red damask doublet, striped hose, mantle in black and gold, fashionably slashed sleeves and, to crown it, a hat with a broad white plume.

"Father!" I greet him. "What a joy to see you! An opportunity, at last, to talk to you, man to man."

He looks me up and down, his face inscrutable.

"In life," I begin, "you always kept well away from me."

No response. But I'm not deterred.

"Say – why were you never there when I needed you? Why did you not take me hunting or jousting, teach me to play tennis or strum the lute? You had plenty of time for other men's offspring. And I was your only child. Why did you fail so miserably in your paternal duties?"

He glares at me, still saying nothing.

"Just let me know this: Why did you marry my mother? There was nothing in it for you. No inheritance, no connections, no advancement... and certainly no love – "

This at last draws a response. Scowling, he reaches for his sword, and I step back, alarmed, until I realise that he can't do anything to hurt me, since I am dead already. He must have come to the same conclusion, for he simply pulls himself up proudly to his full height and growls: "That's enough impudence from you, young man!"

How bizarre to be addressed thus by a man more than two score years my junior! I feel like impressing upon him that I have decades more to my credit than he can boast, but then I'm struck by an intriguing reflection: both my parents ended their days on the scaffold, yet neither has appeared to me in the garb of a prisoner faced with the executioner's axe. On the contrary, I've seen them in full splendour, at the height of their powers. It can only mean that I'm recalling my own impression of them, the image each has left in my memory. By the same standard, my father is seeing, not a seventy-eight-year-old highly respected clergyman, but the awkward ten-year-old of our last meeting.

Aware of the strength of his intellect, I can't wait to discuss this phenomenon with him. But regrettably, he has stomped off, back into the darkness surrounding us.

So I'm no wiser. Still, one resource remains to me: the clever one, who feared neither trolls nor the devil. She if anyone will have the facts worked out for herself, as well as the courage to face them. I always had great admiration for my Aunt Nan, who became Queen
Anne of England.

As before, my thought is enough for her to take shape before me. Strikingly graceful with her delicate features and long slender neck (oh Lord, her neck!), and at the same time regal, imperious. Except she is not in her regalia: no crown, no ermine, no costly jewellery. She is more as I remember her from home: in a soft damask gown and with her French hood of the kind she introduced at court: crescent-shaped, of black velvet, edged with pearls and trimmed with golden gauze. And look – she is wearing a falconer's gauntlet, on which perches, hooded and sedate, Davy, her merlin.

She comes up to stroke my cheek, a familiar glint of mischief in those slanting black eyes that could look right through a person, making them shrink even in their own eyes, though for me they never held anything but affection.

"My dear Jojo," she smirks. "What are you after?"

I decide to leave my parents out of it for the time being. Instead, remembering that, to her, I may still be ten years old, I try an innocent, naïve approach.

"Were you really a witch?"

That makes her smile broader, showing her white even teeth. "Wouldn't you like to know?"

"Is that how you enchanted the King? Through witchcraft?"

"Wouldn't you like to know?"

She was always a terrible one for teasing.

"Yes, my dear aunt, I would like to know. How did you manage to win his love, keep him enthralled, through seven long years? Wasn't it you who got him to break with Rome? Banish his lawfully wedded wife, execute anyone standing in his way, all to make you Queen of England? How did you do it, say? Was it through some magic power of yours?"

All it yields is the same: "Wouldn't you like to know?"

I forget about being ten years old. "But then, how come you didn't play your cards better? How could you let him out of your clutches? Allow him to destroy you – along with four others?"

The grin slides off her face. "That's what I'd like to know."

"Were you guilty of those charges for which you lost your head? Adultery with all those men, incest with your own brother?"

This has her seriously perturbed. Even Davy wakes up and flaps his wings.

"How can you ask such a thing?" she exclaims, and with that, she, too, retreats into the gloom behind her.

I heave a deep sigh. Why are they all so unhelpful? Can it be that they are as ignorant as I am? Flitting around as restless spirits in a vain search for the same? The truth, as we all know, is notorious for putting up resistance.

As I ponder this, it occurs to me that perhaps I should have gone straight to the top.

The king himself will be the one in possession of all the answers. So I call out:

"Your Majesty! King Henry the Eighth of England! I challenge you to appear!"

He doesn't.

I go on, addressing thin air:

"Your Highness – I'm sure you're around. No one is immune to the powers of the spirit. So step forward! This is your chance to come clean!"

Still no sign of him.

"Come on, Henry," I persist. "You can't be far away. There is no need to be coy. Here we are beyond blame and shame, beyond the power and vainglory of the world. And we don't stand on ceremony – one spirit is as good as another. That's why I call you Henry. I hope you don't mind."

He doesn't appear. But just in case he is lurking somewhere nearby, eavesdropping without making himself known, I continue: "What I want to know is this: How did a man like you, fond as you were of carnal pleasures, manage to stay chaste for seven long years waiting for Anne to let you into her bed? Only to have her executed, a mere three years later – this woman you had sacrificed everything for?"

And then, after waiting another moment in vain:

"Finally, Henry – what happened to the romantic, chivalrous knight the world once knew? To the chaste, patient lover of Anne Boleyn? How did he become a brutal murderous tyrant, feared and abhorred far and wide? You can't be the only person in history to have gone through such a fearful transformation. But by God, I wish I knew how these things come about."

The silence is beginning to get on my nerves.

"Answer me, Henry!" I bellow. "You know the reasons, you must do! You have no right to keep them to yourself! By all that is holy I command you: Answer me now!"

No good. She must have got it wrong, the little old woman in Yoxall, when she assured me that all is possible here under this clear light. It appears that spirits are as loath as anyone to answer questions head-on. Or can it be that I misunderstood her? Am I going about it in the wrong way?

Dejected, I look around. Seeing only light but nothing illuminated. But then I hear a voice coming from the shadows. No more than a whisper, but it sounds like my beloved Aunt Mary.

"Jojo," it hisses. "You have to go back."

"Go back?" I repeat. "How can I go back from here?"

"Back to where it all started."

"Where did it start? When?"

The words waft towards me like a cool breeze from the murky surroundings.

"Hever. Christmas.1525."

I am reminded that we are beyond time and place.

Hever Castle

Christmas Day 1525.

Hever. The solar where I spent much of my childhood, when not hovering around the kitchen hoping for titbits from the maids. It was the room to which we all gravitated, the cosiest, most comfortable part of an ancient castle that remained damp and chilly for much of the year. How familiar it all is: the fire burning brightly in the massive fire-place under the Boleyn coat of arms... mullioned windows, colourful wall-hangings... broad floor planks worn down where feet were most wont to tread...

Facing west, the solar got the best of the afternoon sun, but this is a bleak winter's day, dim light filtering in through the leaded window-panes, suggesting a freezing fog of the kind that often came creeping up from the moat in winter-time. It is supposed to be Christmas, but there is little evidence of the festive season: nothing much in the way of decorations, no evergreens, no sweet-smelling herbs on the window-sills. Even the rushes on the floor look limp and scruffy.

And there is my mother, as a young woman, handsome as they say she once was, her face still a blank page, bearing only a trace of the discontent that soon came to leave its mark. She is fair and blue-eyed, neat and well-dressed, in a deep red garment enhancing her pale skin. Perched on an oak stool, she is struggling over a pair of knitting needles, like someone not good with her hands. Anne was the one with nimble fingers, able to produce the most intricate embroidery. She is over on a bench by the bay window, trying to catch the best of the light, while working away at some small linen garment.

Even at this age Anne is, if not exactly beautiful, certainly striking with her erect, slim figure, dark hair and those piercing black eyes. The years in France have taught her all about fashion: she is wearing an elegant low-cut gown of emerald green brocade with the usual matching French hood. She'd make an impression anywhere.

But how come they're both so gloomy? Why this blatant lack of Christmas cheer?

Only Mary seems to be thriving, leisurely enthroned on the one upholstered easy-chair, more splendidly attired than the other two and sucking indulgently at an orange. She looks young, radiant and luscious, notwithstanding the fact that she is heavily pregnant. If this is 1525, she must be expecting Henry, the cousin born less than a year after me.

My eye is drawn towards a wooden cradle tucked away in a corner. In it is a puny infant staring morosely at a spot on the coffered ceiling. Goodness – that can only be me. My very first Christmas.

As the bells of the nearby chapel start to chime, Urian the wolfhound, who has been snoozing contentedly at Anne's feet, sits up and howls in unison.

"Time to pray!" Anne announces. She throws down her needlework and scurries over to a spot of soft rushes, where she gets down on her knees. She clasps her hands, rolls her eyes to heaven and intones in mock – very mock – piety:

"My dear Saint Katherine,
Oh come to myne aid,
And vow that I won't have
To die an old maid.
A husband, Saint Katherine,
A good one, Saint Katherine –
But anyone's better than no one, Saint Katherine.
Please Saint Katherine,
Sweet Saint Katherine,
Handsome Saint Katherine,
Soon Saint Katherine!"

Absorbed in her knitting, Jane takes no notice, but Mary claps her hands, laughing heartily.

"Bravo, Nan! She's bound to heed that!"

"She'd better," says Anne, getting to her feet, "before I die of boredom."

Jane is quick to agree, saying she has never known a more tedious Christmas. No music, no singing, no minstrels, no dancing...

Anne joins in: "No hunting, no hawking, no feasting, no pageantry ... And not a man in sight!"

So where are the men? I wonder. Celebrating in style with the king at court, leaving the women to their own devices?

"Here I am, a married woman," Jane mutters, "lingering like an old spinster with only knitting to entertain me."

"Well at least you have a husband," Anne points out.

"Much good he is to me!"

"Oh stop grumbling you two!" Mary exhorts them. "You are supposed to keep me company, cheer me up for not being allowed at court!"

"It's all right for you," says Anne. "You have both a husband and a lover and a new baby on the way – "

"No wonder she's so smug," This from Jane.

" – while the man I love," Anne continues, "is shackled to a woman he loathes."

"Oh Nan," sighs Mary, "it's time you gave up moaning about Percy. He's not the only man in the world. Personally, I find him quite feeble."

"Percy is not feeble!" Anne snaps, red blooms suddenly appearing on her cheeks. "He was my soul mate. Unlike the other inane courtiers, he had depth."

This brings a joyless laugh from Jane.

"Depth enough to drag you down. See where it landed you."

"That was Wolsey's fault!" Anne retorts. "The insidious schemer, all out to thwart me!"

"You flatter yourself, Nan," says her sister-in-law. "To Cardinal Wolsey you were of no account."

"It's all thanks to him that I'm rotting away here."

Jane's raised eyebrow shows she's unconvinced.

"Wolsey," Anne goes on, "was determined to see Percy married to the daughter of his neighbour up north – "

Uninterested, Jane returns to her knitting needles.

But Anne won't let go of the subject. " – to strengthen defences along the Scottish border. In case of another rebellion."

"Well that wasn't unreasonable," counters her sister-in-law.

As Anne glowers, at her most irascible, Mary intervenes to deflect the course this conversation is taking.

"There is always James Butler," she says equably.

"Never!" her sister cries.

"Anyone's better than no one?"

Anne goes up to stand in front of Mary.

"I was a star in Mechelen at the age of ten. Queen Claude's favourite at Blois. A celebrated newcomer at King Henry's court. Even Lord Percy was a step down for me – "

"A step down?" Jane scoffs. "Heir to the richest family in England?"

"For his sake I was prepared to consider a quiet life in Northumberland. But how anyone could expect me to be buried alive in Ireland – with a man I had never set eyes on – just to solve a squabble over some useless bog land – "

"You never know," says her sister soothingly. "James may be ravishing – those wild Irish looks…"

"I will not be treated like a piece of merchandise!"

"Nan – " Jane resumes, clicking away at her needles. "You think too highly of yourself. Pride has no place in a woman's life."

Mary agrees. "Only when we are loved, can we afford that luxury."

"Exactly," Anne concludes. "I shall only marry for love."

And with that she sits down sullenly, picks up the piece she's been working on, and starts stitching determinedly.

A squeal issues from the cradle: the incumbent, in other words me, likely rattled by the sound of their heated exchange. I watch with interest, wondering how long it will take my mother to respond. She doesn't. It is Mary who gets up from the comfort of her chair, waddles across to rock the cradle, talking to me softly, until I drift off to sleep.

On her way back to the chair, Anne holds out the finished article: a tiny baby shirt with an embellished ruff. Mary examines it, nodding approvingly.

"It's *broderie de l'aiguille*," Anne informs her, clearly pleased with her handiwork. "Queen Claude's favourite stitch. We used to work on it together."

"Well you knew just how to get into her good books. But I do admit – this is exquisite, Nan. Fit for a prince."

"Hardly a prince," says Jane.

"Oh I can tell," Mary states contentedly. "From the way he's kicking. This is no princess."

"It's a bastard."

Mary is not offended.

"A royal bastard, if you please. As the king's son, he will be endowed with wealth, land and titles. And since Queen Catherine has failed to produce a male heir…"

She gives her belly a friendly pat.

Jane reminds her that, even as a royal bastard, he won't be the first in line.

"You mean Bessie Blount's boy? Well that little fellow is already a duke. And Bessie meant nothing to the king."

"Who says?"

"The king himself," Mary informs her. "He only took up with Bessie Blount because, hearing about all King Francis' mistresses, he felt a bit inept not having one himself."

Anne contends that Bessie Blount probably wasn't the first, but Mary says she's pretty sure this was the case. In the early days, she reveals confidentially, being in bed with the king was like having to seduce a virgin.

"A virgin? The king?" Jane sounds incredulous. "What about all the queen's miscarriages, what about the little prince who died? And what about Princess Mary? Are you telling me they were virgin births?"

Mary titters. "I believe they were all modestly conceived by two bashful innocents doing their bit for the monarchy."

The other two look doubtful.

"That it brought little pleasure," Mary expounds, "is borne out by the fact that, as soon as the queen was past child-bearing, he never went near her again."

"But then he had Bessie Blount," says Anne.

"She can't have got very far with him either. It was left to me to convince him that between lovers, untrammelled lust can be both beautiful and romantic."

"Well who better to instruct him?" her sister comments drily.

Jane seems to have lost interest in this lewd conversation. She is concentrating on her knitting. It appears to be coming to an end, she is casting off. Then she holds up a tiny bonnet and hands it to Mary, who peers at it critically.

"This is much too small!"

"Is he going to be that big-headed?"

From a pile of oranges in a bowl on the table, Mary picks up a fruit and fits the bonnet on to it.

"Look – it hardly even fits the orange."

Anne, too, comes up to inspect the bonnet, shaking her head. "Oh Jane – you could have done with a few lessons from Queen Claude. She would have wept if she saw this. You'll have to unravel it and start again."

She throws the bonnet back to Jane, who doesn't bother to catch it. More interested in the orange, she asks if she can have it. Mary tells her she may not, the oranges have been sent to her by the king, for her and her baby. For their health, to ward off the plague.

"But you have so many! Surely you can spare one?"

"I wouldn't mind an orange," says Anne.

"Oh well," Mary concedes, "see who can catch it."

She tosses the orange high in the air. Anne catches it first but Jane tries to snatch it from her, claiming she asked for it first. A tussle ensues.

Elizabeth, mother of Mary, Anne and George, now enters the solar: an impressive woman, endowed with all the stature common to women of high birth. She looks, appalled, at the two young women locked in combat over an orange.

"Girls!" she calls out. "Are you out of your senses? Fighting like cats!"

"These two," Mary says dismissively, "have never learnt the art of sharing. For goodness' sake, have half each!"

Anne peels the orange and gives half to Jane. They go on to eat it, but without much pleasure.

To lighten up the mood, Elizabeth enjoins her younger daughter to lay a star for each one of them for the New Year.

Anne, known for her uncanny ability with cards, locates a deck and picks out the four queens to determine who corresponds to what suit. She holds out the cards first to Mary, who draws one and smiles broadly at the sight of the Queen of Hearts. She holds the card out to show the others.

"What else?" Jane mutters.

Then Anne draws the Queen of Diamonds. "How very apt," she congratulates herself.

"Stylish, clever, confident – "

"And anything but modest," puts in Jane.

Then it's Elizabeth's turn. She draws the Queen of Clubs. Anne nods approvingly.

"Sensible, capable, practical mother. Keeping us all in line."

She hands the last card to Jane.

"Queen of Spades for you, Jane. Sombre, sinister, glum."

"That's not fair!" Jane protests. "I never got to choose!"

"Well someone has to be the last."

"Why always me?"

"Only for now," Mary placates her. "Come on, Nan, let us see what Fate has in store for us all."

Having laid out the four queens in the shape of a cross, Anne shuffles the deck and adds one card on top of each queen.

"The King of Spades for you, Mary. That's not so good."

"A king on top of me is always good," Mary sniggers.

"And mother – you have a Five of Spades. That means passing troubles."

"All troubles have a tendency to pass," Elizabeth comments equably. "That's the only good thing about them."

Jane wants to know what lies ahead for her. She gets a Two of Clubs, which Anne dismisses as "pretty innocuous". Then she places a card over her own queen and grins when she sees the King of Hearts.

At this point, the fortune-telling session comes to a sudden end, as Urian the wolfhound sits up, pricks up his ears and lets out a single resonant bark as a way of announcing an imminent arrival. The next moment hoofbeats are heard. The sound draws an instant response from the four women: as if summonsed, they all rush over to the bay window, craning their necks to see through the dim light who's approaching on the road from the west.

Anne sees them first.

"It's father! And George!"

"What a surprise," says Elizabeth. "Riding all the way from Eltham...?"

In the solar the mood has changed to one of joyful anticipation. Anne is delighted, her black eyes glittering.

"I bet George is bringing my merlin," she beams. "He's promised me a merlin for my New Year present."

"Has he now?" Jane sounds envious.

Mary, too, is grinning happily. "I'm sure they have come with a message," she tells the others. "For me. From the king. I bet he can't bear to be without me any longer."

By the time the hoofbeats have come to a halt in the inner courtyard and hasty steps are heard mounting the spiral stairs to the solar, the four women are lined up facing the door. All, even Jane, are smiling broadly in welcome. Aligned with them, having caught the expectant mood, is Urian, ears pricked, tail wagging.

The two men enter. Their mantles and boots are splashed with mud, their weather-beaten faces set, grim and irate. They scowl at the women, who look back at them, anxious and bewildered. No one speaks. With mounting fury, the men home in on Mary.

She backs away fearfully.

The last thing I hear is a fresh yowl from the cradle.

This, I must say, is intriguing. I never put any credence to the rumours that Mary had once been the king's sweetheart. That my cousin, young Henry, could be anything but the son of her lawfully wedded husband, William Carey. All I know about this uncle of mine by marriage is that he was a distant relation of the king: a favoured, although impoverished, gentleman of the Privy Chamber. It was perhaps thanks to Mary that he was elevated to Esquire of the Body: the groom who helped dress the king and slept on pallet at the foot of his bed – one way of ensuring he was not in bed with his wife! One can only hope alternative accommodation was provided for the nights Mary spent in the king's bed.

What did William make of his wife's adultery? Was he, as an inveterate courtier, prepared to accept the king's intervention as par for the course, a way of improving his own standing at court? If he depended financially on the king's favour, he wouldn't have had any say in the matter. But how did it affect him? Was he left broken-hearted? Mary would have been easy to love.

Now – if my cousin Henry really was the king's son, how come he was never recognized as such? His Majesty never tried to cover up the fact that Bessie Blount's son was his own flesh and blood, if anything, he seemed to take pride in it. There was even speculation at court that the boy was being groomed to succeed his father, in the absence of a legitimate male heir to the throne.

Rumours of Mary's liaison with the king were hotly denied within the family. After I first heard talk about it amongst the servants, I took it up with my grandmother, who was quick to dismiss it as idle gossip. So much nonsense is prated at court, she said, simply to stave off boredom. "There are even those who claim that *I* was once in the king's bed." She rolled her eyes and pulled a wry face. "I could just see myself!" We both burst out laughing at this absurdity. My grandmother: stately, dignified, often intimidating – definitely not a candidate for royal bedhopping.

She never let anyone forget that she descended from one of England's noblest families: the Howards, Dukes of Norfolk. Considering her background, it was surprising that she had been allowed to marry a man who was so far beneath her, though it may have helped that her father was a spendthrift with a gaggle of daughters all requiring a dowry. And Thomas Boleyn's talents superseded his lack of lineage. He wouldn't have been so successful as a diplomat, had he not been endowed with exceptional charm, wit, grace and good manners, enough to outshine most high-born men at court. It is to Elizabeth's credit that she had valued character – combined, admittedly, with Boleyn wealth – above titles and privilege.

Whether or not hers was a love match, her children were not afforded such freedom.

They had spouses chosen for them, I imagine by their ambitious father: a Groom of the Privy Chamber for Mary; Jane, for whatever reason, for George. And James Butler for Anne, to settle an Irish land dispute.

What if Anne had agreed to marry James Butler? What a difference it would have made, to her life, to the life of us all, to King Henry VIII, to England, to the whole world as we know it! The king and his chancellor Cardinal Wolsey were both in favour of the match, thinking it would appease an unruly Irish clan and help quell the on-going threat of Irish rebellion.

But Anne had different ideas.

So it was Wolsey who had put paid to her romance with Percy, leaving my aunt irate and despondent, indefinitely rusticated. She, who had never been prepared, or intended, for a life of quiet domesticity in the country. All she could hope for now was for some man to appear, like a *deus ex machina*, to transform her life. Her glorious inculcation in three different royal households, coupled with her own splendid qualities, were no use to her, or anyone else, without a man to release them. But where would she find one, alone with a few servants at Hever, while the rest of the family enjoyed the trappings of life at court?

The one I can't work out at all is my mother. By this time, she would have had every reason to count her blessings. Her knight in shining armour had appeared on his proverbial white charger, furnished her with, not only a handsome young husband with a promising future ahead, but also with all she could wish for in terms of comfort, security and position, and a healthy baby to boot. Yet in the scene I just witnessed, she showed no sign of pleasure or gratitude. The venom of discontent seeped out each time she opened her mouth. What made her so rancorous? Did she have something wrong with her?

After my mother died, I made some enquiries into her family background. Though I had never been in contact with any of them, I reckoned there had to be grandparents, aunts, uncles, cousins, and I nursed a vain hope that, at some stage, their paths would cross mine.

I did discover that my maternal grandfather, Lord Morley, was a respected but penniless baron, a second cousin of the king. As contemporaries, he and young Prince Henry had been brought up together under the supervision of their joint grandmother, born as Margaret Beaufort. Their education was strictly devout, as she herself was deeply religious – in my own college, she was held up as a paragon of profound piety, on par with a saint. Their shared childhood had created a bond of sorts between the king and my grandfather, leading in due course to a court appointment for Lord Morley as a gentleman usher and a position for his eldest daughter in Queen Catherine's household.

Lord Morley was known to be an erudite scholar more interested in books and learning than in the vacuous formality of court life. I suppose it's him I take after. If we had ever met, we might have found many a common interest.

If I know little about Jane's father, I know even less about her mother. Apart from the odd appearance at court, Lady

Morley seems to have preferred living quietly at the family manor in Norfolk, while other members of her family enjoyed life in London. My mother, to her credit, used her position to benefit her younger siblings: brother Henry was knighted on the occasion of Anne's coronation, and a marriage was arranged between her sister Margaret and a Boleyn cousin, John Shelton, heir to great wealth.

Otherwise, she had little to spare for the Boleyns, including my own self, who saw little of my mother even on the rare occasions when she put in an appearance at Hever. Once when I was quite young, I overheard my grandmother upbraiding her for neglecting her maternal duties. To that she replied that, as far as she was concerned, her duties lay with her sovereign, Queen Catherine.

Oh yes, Queen Catherine. A tragic figure. For nearly twenty years our proud, undisputed sovereign – only to find herself, in her early forties, obsolete and discarded, having failed at her main assignment: to produce a male heir. I'm reminded of Mary's appraisal of the royal couple's intimate relations. The queen would have been brought up according to royal Spanish tradition: to be above all virtuous, chaste and devout. If it had been drummed into her from the start that carnal knowledge was for the sole purpose of procreation... and if each encounter carried a risk of yet another abortive pregnancy, for which she felt physically and mentally unprepared... What degree of pleasure could be expected?

His Majesty's liaison with Mary would have offered him something quite different. I see my aunt before me, as she was that Christmas Day at Hever: in her full bloom of youth – so sweet and oh so delectable... I can well imagine the king losing his heart to her. It begs the question:

How could he ever stop loving her?

A London Tavern

Christmas Day 1525

But where are we now? Not at Hever, for sure. It looks like a tavern, one of those rough London hostelries along the Thames that I have heard exist but never dreamt of frequenting. It's packed with a crowd of noisy thugs in an advanced state of inebriation calling out Christmas greetings to one another. What an extraordinary way of celebrating the birth of our Saviour!

The air is a fetid miasma, thick with the stench of stale beer, unwashed bodies and worse. Many of the patrons are poorly dressed for winter weather, some are in rags — more prone, I should think, to spend the few pennies they have on beer rather than a new pair of breeches or clogs. In amongst the men are a few women: the kind, I presume, who have no homes to go to or families to tend. At least a festive atmosphere prevails, going to some extremes: one fellow is vomiting into a booth to the consternation of an amorous couple ensconced there; another, relieving himself out of a window, straight into the river, is met by a torrent of abuse from a hapless oarsman passing by below.

Dear God. What am I doing here?

A man enters carrying a lute. He is in plain dark clothing, with a black woollen cap pulled down over his brow. Even so, the easy confidence of his movement indicates more of a gentleman. The crowd seem to notice the same, for they pull away from him suspiciously. It is obvious that this is not a character they are used to seeing around.

The fellow finds himself a rough-hewn three-legged stool and pulls it out on to the floor. The others edge away. As he sits down and starts tuning his lute, he attracts a certain interest. But when the tuning goes on for an inordinately long time, the onlookers lose patience.

"Play on willya!" cries a hoarse voice.

"Yeah," growls another. "Wha' ave you to sing for us?"

The lute-player gives a complicit smile suggesting he has something very special on offer.

"'Ave ye 'erd the ballad abou' Mary Bullen?"

I'm struck by two considerations: One, that his vernacular sounds terribly contrived. Two, that the name of my Aunt Mary ought not to be mentioned in a place like this.

"C'mon then!" someone shouts. "Give us the one abou' Mary Bullen!"

"Yeah!" another joins in. "Less 'ear!"

And so the singing starts:

> *"'Er father took her off to France,*
> *at court 'er to install.*
> *'E never thought she'd end up as*
> *the greatest 'ore of all."*

The shouting has stopped. Heed is being paid, heads are turned to the singer, as he breaks into a refrain:

> *"Mary Bullen is the greatest,*
> *Mary Bullen is the greatest,*
> *Mary Bullen is the greatest,*
> *she's the greatest 'ore of all!"*

A filthy lout, leering with a single tooth in his upper jaw, repeats the last words, harshly, out of tune: "She's the gweatest 'ore of all!"

I'm aghast. How can this be possible? A lovely decent woman like my precious Aunt Mary made the object of such nefarious attention – in an establishment of this order, amongst such company! Someone is obviously out to hurt her. Has she made herself so hated at court? Are other women envious of her having the king's favour? Or are there worse, sinister forces at play?

The lyrics have swept away any reservations among the audience. Relishing their attention, the balladeer forgets about his cockney accent and continues with every 'h' in place:

"King Francis took her maidenhead,
  he taught her to play ball.
  Then passed her round his courtiers,
  the greatest whore of all."

The one-toothed lout waves his arms, encouraging the crowd to sing along:

"Mary Bullen is the greatest,
  Mary Bullen is the greatest,
  Mary Bullen is the greatest,
  she's the greatest whore of all!"

Tankards are no longer lifted. They all pay rapt attention, as I do myself, to the ballad's third verse:

"Sir Thomas had to call her back,
  her debauchery to stall.
  But London made no diff'rence to
  the greatest whore of all."

There are foolish smiles on all faces. With no need for further encouragement, a host of raucous voices join in the chorus:

"Mary Bullen is the greatest,
  Mary Bullen is the greatest,
  Mary Bullen is the greatest,
  she's the greatest whore of all!"

I can only hope this loathsome ballad never went any further than these sordid walls –
    God forbid that it ever reached the ears of the king!

Someone brings a filled tankard to the balladeer. He takes a few deep draughts and then goes on:

"King Henry soon set eyes on her.
He couldn't help but fall.
He didn't realise she was
the greatest whore of all."

Again, they all sing, if you can call it that. It's more like the baying of a pack of hounds – with severely afflicted throats:

"Mary Bullen is the greatest,
Mary Bullen is the greatest,
Mary Bullen is the greatest,
she's the greatest whore of all!"

A shrill woman's voice pipes up: "The greatest 'ore of all!" followed by a man's voice: "Speak fer yersen!" It gives rise to cascades of raw laughter.

Do they not realise that singing, even hearing, this foul ballad makes them all guilty of treason, punishable by execution? Spreading vile slander... hideous lies, designed to cause the worst possible damage to the reputation of a pure innocent woman...

And there is still worse to come:

"The king believes the child is his,
But scores of men recall
her opening her legs to them,
the greatest whore of all."

And then the chorus is repeated, twice for good measure:

"Mary Bullen is the greatest,
Mary Bullen is the greatest,

Mary Bullen is the greatest,
she's the greatest whore of all!"

Slowly, amid loud cheers and laughter, the tavern fades away.

Hever Castle

Christmas Day 1525.

Back at Hever, thank goodness. The solar, looking much as before, except it is later in the day: darkness has fallen, two candles flicker on the window-sill. Only two people are in the room: Mary, no longer in proud command on the easy-chair but pitifully slumped on a bench, shrunk back into herself. Towering above her is Elizabeth, looking ruefully at her daughter, holding something like a parchment in her right hand.

"Oh Mary!" She shakes her head. "What you have done to destroy this family."

"I haven't done anything!" Mary objects feebly.

"Your father no longer Treasurer of the Household. Your brother banished from the Privy Chamber – "

"It was all thanks to me that they got those appointments."

"We're all finished at court."

Mary makes a brave attempt to straighten herself up.

"I'll put it right again, mother. As soon as my little baby is born – "

"Don't fool yourself," her mother says. "The King will never forgive you."

"He loves me!" Mary vows. "He'll come round."

Elizabeth brushes that away.

"The King loves no one but himself."

Mary makes another attempt to defend herself.

"No one cares for him as I do. I know what's behind those royal trappings."

Elizabeth nods. "Indeed. There is a lot to King Henry that his subjects are unaware of.

"At times he's not like a king at all," Mary muses. "When he's worried about state affairs... He gets terrible headaches..."

"That's because his head was never intended for the crown," her mother reminds her.

"The same goes for his heart," Mary adds tenderly. "That's why he's so content with me. In my arms he can forget all about being regal and imperious. He knows that seeing him shy and insecure only makes my heart grow fonder."

Elizabeth knows better.

"No man wants to be loved for his weakness. Men want to be loved for their strength. To the king you were a foil showing him off to the world as a romantic, chivalrous knight. A role his poor ageing queen was no longer able to fulfil."

Mary allows herself a faint smile.

"I love that side of him too."

"But it's all over now." Elizabeth holds the parchment out like a foul, evil-smelling rag. "The vile allegations of this ballad... out all over London. You've seen them yourself. How do you think the king reacted when they were brought to his attention? He's been made to appear a fool. A cuckold."

"It's all lies!" Mary tells her, her eyes brimming with tears. "I've never been anything but faithful! Since the first time he took me to his bed I haven't set eyes on another man!"

"What's of concern to the king," says her mother, "is how other men see him. To have been hoodwinked into romancing – even loving – the King of France's cast-off whore... Francis of all people!"

Now Mary is weeping, as she has good reason to.

"You make it sound so ugly!" she sobs. "I'm not a bad person. I just happened to fall in love with a king."

"Come, Mary," says Elizabeth. "We all know what you got up to in France. You were a wanton and rejoicing in it. God alone knows what would have become of you if we hadn't brought you back and set you up with a decent husband."

Mary's face is awash with tears.

"What was I to do?" she weeps. "I was thirteen years old. Dumped at the French court where men were after one thing only. Commanded by the King of France into his royal bed. Who was I to refuse?"

"Well Nan did and got away with it."

"That's only because she was under the wing of Queen Claude! You should have let me come back with Princess Mary! After she left, I had no one. No father, no mother to protect me. No brother, not a single friend. Abandoned in a foreign country – I couldn't even speak the language. I was so lonely!"

Mary's loud sobbing cuts no ice with her mother.

"Did you really think that making yourself available to droves of French courtiers would act as a cure for loneliness?"

"At least they wanted me!" Mary cries out. "Even if it was only for a night! Even if it was only for my body! At least they wanted me! No one else did!"

Elizabeth is contemplating her, still void of sympathy.

"How much had you told King Henry about your exploits in France?"

"Well he was always keen to hear details of life at the French court..."

"I'm talking about your own loose morals."

"I couldn't tell him about that! He assumed I was a virgin when I married William."

"Well the ballad has put paid to that illusion. Your French reputation has caught up with you. A gift to a balladeer. And to all our enemies at court."

In the silence that follows, Mary looks down at her bulging stomach.

"My baby!" she exclaims. "What will become of my baby?"

Her mother is under no illusion.

"King Henry will never recognize your child. Not with a doubt of paternity hanging over it."

"But he knows..." Mary tries to convince herself. "I swear it could only be his! I haven't been near anyone else! Not even my husband."

"That is neither here nor there."

Mary still clings to a hope.

"Once the king learns the truth..."

"In court circles," her mother interrupts her, "the truth is immaterial. What matters is what people think."

"I will put everything right!" Mary persists. "The king will listen. I'll reassure him. As soon as I'm back at court."

"No, Mary," says Elizabeth. "You're not going back to court. Not now. Not ever."

And she adds darkly: "You've done enough damage."

At some point I heard Elizabeth mention Eltham. That rings a bell... What have I read about Eltham? Eltham Palace...? Of course. The Eltham Ordinances: an initiative by Cardinal Wolsey to make sweeping changes to the organisation of the king's household. Cost-cutting measures had to be introduced, as the coffers of the crown were being seriously depleted by the king's extravagant life-style, not to mention the costly wars with France.

What a godsend for the cardinal! A royal licence to dispense of all threats to his own authority: the hateful courtiers close to the king, whose rise to power he had been watching with jealousy and genuine concern.

Pieces are beginning to fall into place. On top of Wolsey's list of undesirables would have been the two Boleyns, *père et fils*. However, the king would never have agreed to dismiss these two favourites from their high offices as long as he remained infatuated with Mary, their daughter and sister. Wolsey's first measure would therefore have been to get her, once and for all, out of the king's bed.

Yes – it had to be Wolsey. I can't think of anyone else with the incentive as well as the wherewithal to send spies out to France to investigate Mary's experiences as a young girl at the French court. And he had struck gold. All the cardinal had to do, once the precious information was received, was to commission the writing of the ballad, have it printed on to parchment and then widely distributed.

My thoughts go back to the too-respectable balladeer, the hat pulled down over his brow, the unconvincing attempts to sound like a cockney.

The ballad fired where it hurt. Wolsey may well have taken it upon himself to inform His Majesty, politely and solicitously, of its existence. He would have known only too well that Henry was wont to measure himself against the King of France, almost to the point of obsession. Had he not been present himself at the spectacle some years before, when King Henry, along with four thousand English guests, attended a meeting with Francis I at the Field of the Cloth of Gold near Calais? Inordinate amounts of English taxpayers' money were spent on a senseless extravaganza of banquets, jousts and revelries, lavishly designed with the sole aim of impressing the French king. All, I've been told, to no avail, as the supercilious Francis looked down his long nose at Henry's lack of sophistication, taking a perverse pride in his own lascivious court, his posse of mistresses and royal bastards.

King Henry with his strict upbringing and religious constraints couldn't possibly match this level of licentiousness. It would have made more sense for him to claim the higher moral ground, set himself up as a royal paragon of virtue. On that score, King Francis would have been hard pushed to remain superior.

How did the king feel, learning about his sweetheart's early indiscretions? If he truly loved her, he might have made an effort to understand how they had come about. But if Elizabeth was right, Mary's role in his life was merely to enhance his own sense of self as well as his public image. Now, with the ballad, he found himself instead ridiculed and reviled. So Mary had to go, her unborn child and her family with her.

Henry only catered to himself. He was the king. He was the one who mattered.

* * *

Memories come flooding back, memories I didn't know I had, some going back as far as my cradle. Maybe all our experiences are lodged deep within us, leaving an indelible imprint on our brain, or rather, our spirit. What now emerges is a fierce row at Hever that must have taken place in early 1526. I was then a mere infant, but I would have been present, and that may be all it takes.

It starts with a distressed Mary calling out in a shrill voice that they can't all go off to London, leaving her there on her own.

Her mother, in an attempt to calm her down, explains that she needs to accompany her husband to court. He needs all the support he can get to regain royal favour.

"That goes for me too!" I hear George booming.

"Well what about Jane?" Mary whines. "She can stay behind with me."

But Jane haughtily informs her that, as lady-in-waiting to Queen Catherine, she has received a royal summons.

"Well then Nan can be here with me!"

"Certainly not!" Anne declares. "I've had enough of rustication!"

"I bet you're hoping to catch the eye of the king," her brother nudges her. "He's bound to suffer pangs of loneliness without the luscious Mary beside him."

"Or rather underneath him," Jane says pointedly.

"Don't you bank on me for the king's favour," Anne tells him. "I'm not stupid like my sister."

"You can't leave me here all alone!" Mary's voice is breaking. "What will I do when the baby comes?"

Mary's concern is not without reason. As I know only too well, few things can be as perilous for a woman as giving birth to a child. With her lying-in being not far off, it is understandable that she wants to have her mother or sister, or preferably both, close by.

Elizabeth points out that she will have the support of her grandmother, who is no stranger to giving birth. In addition, a good midwife will be found in London and dispatched together with a suitable wet-nurse.

Mary reluctantly agrees, as long as she can come straight back to court once she is over the birth.

"My dear girl," says her mother. "We've made it clear that you are not going back to court."

"I'm not staying here!" Mary cries. "Not on my own! What would I do with myself?"

Elizabeth suggests drily that she can start by taking care of her children.

"A nursemaid? Is that all I'm good for?"

"Yes, Mary," says her mother. "You may as well get used to the idea."

And that's how it ends.

Mary's downfall became my good fortune, for I couldn't have wished for a better mother to replace my own. Lacking other diversions, she devoted herself to the care of her two children and me. Once young Henry was born, she insisted on nursing him herself – even I was occasionally allowed a drop of her milk. She never made me feel I was anything but her own.

I can see the four of us together: days of early summer spent on a sward down by the river, water glittering under a blazing sun... Mary extended on a rug wearing only her chemise, her hair loose, her skin exposed... the scent of wild flowers, fresh grass and sun-baked earth... the buzzing of bees and singing of larks mingling with her peals of laughter as we clambered all over her, like cubs on a Mammy Bear.

And then cold and dark winter evenings, curled up on soft velvet cushions in front of a blazing fire in the nursery, enjoying mugs of hot milk and cinnamon rusks, while Mary entertained us with tales passed down by her grandmother: of knights and ladies, chivalry and romance. We were too young to follow much of the action, but the soothing sound of Mary's voice lulled us to sleep, so that often we had to be roused to be put to bed.

Every now and then Mary returned to the nursery in the dead of night to collect one of us, I imagine to stave off her loneliness. There was a spell – while Kitty was going through a period of being particularly obstreperous and young Henry was still just a bundle of wet nappies – when I was the lucky one chosen to share her bed, Oh the bliss of going to sleep in the warmth of her soft embrace! I had to wait half a life-time before I experienced anything like it again.

If Mary hankered for the intimacy of a lover, I think the physical closeness she experienced with us children made up for at least some of it. And we did our best to stop her brooding. Whenever we caught her day-dreaming, gazing morosely into the distance, her eyes misting over, we'd compete to gain her attention. Kitty with her madcap ways did her best to make her laugh. I was better at asking questions, getting answers that were sometimes hard to understand.

I got on well with my cousin Kitty. A year older than me, she took on the role as our natural leader. From an early age she knew how to use her talents to get others to dance to her tune. In this she did not take after her mother, who was entirely lacking in guile. Kitty was more like our Aunt Nan.

There came a time when I lost my place uppermost in Mary's heart. She no longer took me to her bed at night but preferred young Henry, who had grown into a delightful toddler, chubby and sweet-natured, as made for hugs and cuddles. His mother was besotted with him. Oddly, I can't remember my youngest cousin as being any older than two or three years of age – it is almost as if he had died in infancy, though I know this not to be the case.

Perhaps it was I who distanced myself from him, out of jealousy? What did I have to offer Mary compared to this smiling, golden-haired cherub? I remained puny, shy and reserved, no doubt due to the fact that, unlike young Henry, who had been embraced with his mother's undying devotion from the first breath he drew, all I had had was the attention of a sullen wet nurse, whose interest in me was limited to the fee she exacted for her milk.

One other member of the family resided at Hever: Grandma Butler, as we called her, though she was really our great-grandmother, mother to our grandfather Thomas. Hever had been her home during her marriage to Thomas' father, and when he died, leaving the castle to his son, she stayed on.

Grandma Butler was of Irish descent, which according to our grandmother Elizabeth explained a lot. She was certainly unusual, bowing to no one, a law on to herself, sustained by the supreme confidence that comes of being born to wealth and nobility. I'm in no doubt that a generous portion of her sturdy Irish blood ran in the veins of her grandchildren Anne and George.

Small and wiry, with piercing black eyes just like Anne's, she gave an impression of seeing and understanding much more than she vented. She made a habit of expressing herself through wry statements that were shrewd and to the point, or pithy aphorisms rife with Celtic wisdom.

Whenever hunger got the better of Grandma Butler and she appeared at mealtimes, we were strictly instructed by Mary to behave impeccably and not annoy her in any way. I couldn't help wondering why both she and our grandfather were so deferential towards this peculiar old woman, but as an adult I found out: Grandma Butler was the one who held the purse strings, a good deal richer than anyone else in the family.

Her father, the seventh Earl of Ormond, finding himself without a male heir, had taken the unusual step of leaving his considerable fortune, in England as well as Ireland, to be shared by his two surviving daughters – an arrangement that met with irate objections from Piers Butler, the Irish claimant to the title. The proposal to marry Anne off to his son and heir, James, had been seen as an expedient solution to the dispute. No one had counted on Anne's stubborn refusal to be "buried alive" in Ireland.

As children we saw little of Grandma Butler. Her domain was a chamber above the estate office, accessible only by stairs located in the west tower. While Mary was welcome to spend time with her there, we were not. She had made it clear that she did not like children, in spite of, or perhaps due to, the fact that she had given birth to no less than ten, before her husband left her widowed with half of them still minors.

The one person she favoured above all others, including the rest of her seven surviving children, was her second son Thomas, our grandfather. On his rare visits to Hever, he spent much of his time closeted in the office with his mother, according to Mary "discussing her affairs".

As the nominated heir to Grandma Butler's fortune, Thomas had taken over the administration of her English property, which included no less than seventy-two manors. He was less concerned with the Irish part of the inheritance, which in his absence Piers Butler had taken command of. However, he did dispute the latter's claim to the title of Earl of Ormond, which he wanted for himself. The king, asked to intervene, diffused the situation by making Piers Butler Earl of Ossory. This title carried less prestige but served to keep the Irishman quiet for the time being. Unrest in Ireland was always a worry.

Our grandmother Elizabeth, of higher rank being the daughter of a premier English duke, did not see any need to defer to Grandma Butler. On her regular visits to Hever, she grumbled about the lackadaisical way the household was run in her absence. Referring to our great-grandmother's total lack of aptitude when it came to housekeeping, she was frequently heard muttering: "We're not in Ireland."

Elizabeth's efforts to raise standards came as a bit of a shock to both us and the household staff, used as we all were to a more lax regime. Mary, bless her heart, was no more suited as a chatelaine – it was a role for which she had never been prepared. We children didn't mind a bit of dirt and disorder, as long as there was food on the table. Mould on the bread we could scrape off, and if the milk was sour, we drank ale instead.

Having said that, we did appreciate the improvements imposed by our grandmother. From the moment she arrived, the castle became a hive of activity: everyone except for Grandma Butler got busy cleaning, tidying and laundering; baking, brewing and cooking. Each one had a task assigned to them. Kitty and I, though hardly more than toddlers, were sent out to weed the garden or pick berries, fruit and vegetables. Women were set spinning, weaving and sewing; our clothes were mended if ripped, replaced if outgrown. Kitty was especially pleased with the new gowns Elizabeth brought her from London.

One time, when I fell ill with fever, my grandmother happened to be in residence, and so it was she who nursed me back to health. I remember waking from a delirium to find her sitting at my bedside, watching over me with an expression of genuine concern. Having satisfied myself that this was not another feverish vision, I managed a weak smile. A glimpse of tenderness washed over her face, and she reached out to gently stroke my cheek. It made me so happy, I would have been content to remain sick for ever.

Daily life at Hever was settled and secure, if somewhat dull. We welcomed the regular arrivals by other family members, their guests and additional servants. Especially anticipated were my father's rare visits. I would drink in the colourful splendour of his apparel: plumed hat, velvet doublet, silk breeches, slashed sleeves and prominent cod-piece. Added to his attractions was the carefree, reckless bearing of a man who had never had to submit or apologize to anyone, bar possibly His Royal Highness. I dreamt of growing up one day to be a man just like him.

My father came to Hever usually in the company of a few distinguished guests. After spending the day out hunting or hawking, they indulged in a lengthy meal in the Great Hall.

On these occasions servants in the kitchen were ordered to pull out all the stops. Once everyone was seated at the long trestle tables, after hands had been washed and grace said, the minstrels started playing and a procession of countless dishes was brought in: spiced lampreys and cold capon, pig and rabbit, beef and mutton, carp and salmon and I don't know what. Kitty and I, once we were old enough to share a seat at the end of the top table, had small helpings while waiting impatiently for the banquet of sweetmeats: spiced custard and almond cream, syllabub and marchpane. At the end of it all, we were each allowed a mouthful of delicious hippocras.

While stuffing my mouth, I would keep my eyes fixed on my father's face, watching him eat and drink, laugh and talk and entertain his guests, all with his usual easy-going charm. Sooner or later, I thought, his gaze would turn in my direction, meet my eye and acknowledge my presence, my perfect behaviour. The slightest sign of approval, a brief nod or a shadow of a smile, would have been enough to satisfy me. But I waited in vain. As far as my father was concerned, I didn't exist.

One winter afternoon, I hatched what I thought was a clever plan. Seeing him take off his big leather boots to warm his feet in front of the large fire-place in the entrance hall, I sneaked in behind him and furtively hid his boots behind a chest. When the time came for him to depart, there was great consternation, as he couldn't find his boots where he had placed them. Servants were called and scolded for having misplaced them. For a while I watched them all searching frantically; then I reckoned my moment of glory had arrived. Like a hero I stepped forward, proudly and wordlessly holding out my father's boots. But no reward or even gratitude was forthcoming; all I got for my effort was a clip around the ear.

Otherwise, the one whose company I came to treasure more and more was Anne. Appearing at Hever for longer or shorter spells, she seemed to have overcome her impatience with country life, happy to lend a hand to the mundane chores of so little appeal to her sister.

Everyone at Hever became more animated by her presence: children, servants, even animals, perked up when she was around. Anne was full of fun, happy to join Kitty and myself playing quoits or hopscotch or teaching us the latest dances from London. When I protested that dancing was only for girls, she said, not at all, at court everyone has to dance, even the cats and dogs. That I could well believe, seeing the excitement of Urian the wolfhound, getting up on his hind legs, barking and wagging his tail, when he saw Anne dance in front of him.

Urian was her special pet. She had got him as a puppy during her lonely days of rustication and, for lack of better things to do, had devoted hours and days training him. He was able to do tricks like no other dog I have ever known, even reading signs giving different commands, like 'SIT', 'DOWN' and 'ROLL', and following suit. Anne used to laugh and say it was only a matter of time before he'd read her prayer book. When she was away at court, often for months on end, Urian hovered sedately close to the gate, no doubt awaiting her return, for he only had to set eyes on her to become once more as lively as a puppy.

And then there was her other favourite: a black stallion called Augustus. While the palfreys kept for ladies at Hever were quiet and biddable, even strong men had trouble controlling Augustus. The grooms complained bitterly about being bitten and kicked and run away with when ordered to exercise him. Only with Anne did he behave impeccably. The grooms stared in wonder as he "came quiet under her hands". Never doubting her command of the horse, she let me as a small child come along for rides, sitting in front of her in the saddle, her arm clasped firmly around my waist. I remember hair-raising gallops, mud splashing my face as I clung to the pommel, breathless and exhilarated, shrieking – with pleasure, not fear – each time Augustus took a flying leap over a fallen tree trunk or puddle.

Anne had an amazing way with animals. Learning from her to understand and respect them fostered in me a life-long affinity with all God's creatures. My life would have been empty without my beloved pets. Like the dog I had in Lichfield, a black and white sheepdog called Bill, who faithfully attended all my services, sitting in a front pew, paying more attention than many of my parishioners, and barking his assent each time he heard the word 'amen'. Some people objected to the dog's presence in the cathedral, but I'm sure the good Lord didn't mind the attendance of man's best friend.

More pertinently, it was Anne who instilled in me a devotion to books, learning and scholarship. On many a rainy day I climbed the stone spiral staircase to her bedchamber, to find her

65

there immersed in a book. She read me passages from the Bible and told me stories from the New Testament, which moved me more deeply than Mary's wild yarns of gallantry and romance. Best of all was being allowed a look at Anne's Book of Hours. Even though I was too young to read, I could pore for hours over its resplendent illustrations and brilliantly illuminated script.

Like all children, I saw my own circumstances as a fair representation of life itself. I was fortunate in having such an idyllic introduction to it. And like all children, I expected it to continue unchanged. As we grow up, we soon discover that there is no such thing as permanence in human affairs – but no one could have imagined the tumult awaiting us at Hever: an irrevocable process already set in train.

Hever Castle

March 1527.

The parlour at Hever: a small chamber off the entrance hall, dim for much of the day, as it's on the west side of the castle. The east side has the well, so that's were the kitchen is.

A fire is blazing merrily in the hearth, and in front of it is my father, sprawled comfortably in an armchair. Still in his riding gear, his face spattered with mud, he must have only just come in. On a table nearby is his plumed hat.

My grandmother enters with a pitcher and two tankards and proceeds to pour each of them some ale.

"This is a surprise," she says. "Aren't you supposed to be with the king at Windsor?"

Her son nods and takes a deep draught of ale, then tells her he had indeed been looking forward to some quiet pastime, sitting down to a game of primero or perhaps chess.

Instead he had to get on his horse and ride post to Hever.

"Whatever for?"

"To ensure you're all prepared," he says, opening his arms in a gesture of mock pomposity, "for the imminent arrival of His Majesty King Henry."

Elizabeth blanches.

"Is he expecting beds for the night? With all his retinue"

"Not at all," her son reassures her. "He's putting up at Bidborough. His visit here will be short and sweet."

"Has Nan been informed?"

Yes, George says, he met her on her way out.

"I handed over the latest royal gift and told her to be damned sure to wear it."

"What is it this time?"

"A gold bracelet with a medallion dangling from it. Portraying none other than Himself."

Elizabeth looks amused. "A constant reminder."

George, too, guffaws.

"On the assumption that she's pining herself sick for his presence."

Sitting back, he runs a hand through his auburn bangs, grown a little too long, giving him an unkempt look.

"When I see how love is affecting the king," he ponders, "I thank my Creator that I was never thus afflicted."

His mother looks at him thoughtfully.

"With Mary at least," she says slowly, "feelings went both ways. Say what you will about your sister, her heart is in the right place. She truly loved His Majesty – not for what he was, but for himself. And she asked for nothing in return but his love."

"Well that," George avows, "is uncommon in court circles, where everyone is out for what they can get."

"His Majesty was devoted to her."

"Like a fool," is George's glib comment.

Elizabeth remains serious.

"Losing Mary the way he did, for the worst of all reasons, must have caused him great hurt. Just as there is no greater joy in life, no better boost to your spirit, than finding yourself loved by someone you adore, few things can be more cruel than losing your faith in the object of your affection. That's worse than losing your loved one to death."

A hint of sadness in her voice suggests that she is speaking from personal experience.

"The king," she tells her son, "wouldn't deign to admit it, but Mary's fall from grace must have left him with a searing wound that could only be healed by someone like her: another Mary but without her flaws; someone as capable of tender loving but with a stainless reputation."

George looks into the fire, smiling to himself.

"When I heard the first intimations at court about the king having a new love interest, I had a feeling it might be our Nan."

"Well I still find it surprising."

"Why? Nan has a lot to recommend her."

"After the blow he had suffered..." His mother frowns, disturbed by the very thought. "Would you not have expected him to distance himself from our family? Seek his new pleasures further afield?"

"As in once bitten, twice shy?"

"The court, as we all know, is swarming with desirable young ladies only too keen to accommodate His Royal Highness. Yet he ended up courting the one who isn't."

George drinks some more ale and then turns to his mother, telling her he knows full well why the king settled for his sister.

"Last month, alone with me in the Privy Chamber at Greenwich, after a huge meal with large quantities of wine consumed, he let slip that he had recently, in a fit of black despondency, gone down on his knees and beseeched the Lord to send him a woman worthy of him."

"After Mary's disgrace?"

"Obviously. For when Nan reappeared at court only a few days later, dazzling him with her style, wit and charm, it left His Highness in no doubt that here was the living answer to his prayer. In his own words he was 'stricken with the dart of love'."

He chortles. "Grandma Butler has warned us to be careful what we pray for."

His mother looks doubtful.

"It's not that simple, George."

She gets up and checks that no one is nearby, then takes care to close the doors leading to the hall and office, as if preparing to say something that could land them both in trouble.

"There is more to King Henry," she begins in a low voice, "than meets the eye. I recall seeing him as a four-year-old taking part in a royal parade, mounted on a massive grey palfrey. My heart went out to the poor child – I could see he was terrified, of falling off his horse, of disgracing himself in front of the crowd, of displeasing his father the king. And most of all, scared that his fear might show…"

"Oh well," says her son dismissively. "That was when he was four years old."

"His parents had no time for him," Elizabeth continues. "Their main concern was to maintain their precarious hold on the throne. Their limited resource of parental attention was devoted to Arthur, priming him for his future role as king. Young Prince Henry was overlooked and neglected, left in the unforgiving hands of his formidable grandmother."

"That old trout! I've heard all about her."

His mother nods pensively. "Margaret Beaufort would have been more intent on instilling the fear of God than indulging her charge with enfeebling affection. She decided that Prince Henry should devote his life to the church."

That brings a burst of laughter from George.

"His Majesty in a pulpit! And a celibate! What a joke!"

"Old King Henry was openly disparaging about his younger son. When Prince Arthur died unexpectedly, leaving ten-year-old Henry heir presumptive, his aggrieved father made no secret of the fact that he found his heir woefully inadequate, lacking the qualities required for kingship."

Her son looks doubtful.

"Most of us agreed. The little we saw of this gawky, overgrown child did not bode well for the future of England. And when Henry VII died suddenly, giving us as king the seventeen-year-old Henry VIII, we held our breath in trepidation."

George grins. "He proved you all wrong, didn't he?"

"Indeed. He had turned into a splendid young knight: tall, broad and disporting. He excelled at hunting and jousting, dancing and playing the lute..."

"What about state affairs?"

"They were left in the hands of Cardinal Wolsey. Who was astute enough to let the king believe he was the one in charge. It left the cardinal free to line his own pockets, while His Majesty amused himself with his favourite pastimes."

"It must have made for jolly times at court."

"Too jolly at times. The king liked to surround himself with pleasure-loving young nobles rather than the stalwart old aristocrats of his father's court..."

"His so-called minions."

"Some of them so wild, they had to be sent back home before they damaged the monarch's reputation. They are still around, and I must admit, in your younger days I had my concerns about you joining that crowd. But father assured me we could rely on you behaving yourself."

George gets up to put another log on the fire, while his mother goes on reminiscing.

"Oh yes. The young king had us all enchanted. Yet underneath the chivalrous manners I detected something like hunger for approval. A desperate need to show all and sundry that he was every bit as good, if not a better king than his brother would have been."

After a brief pause she adds:

"I think that's why he married Arthur's widow."

"I've been told he was after the unpaid Spanish dowry."

"That as well. Still, the marriage was quite successful. There was obvious affection between husband and wife. And with the young king's gargantuan appetite for all the good things in life, he is sure to have enjoyed his early conjugal life. One pregnancy followed another. Just a pity that all they produced was a daughter."

George shrugs. "And then one day his queen was past it, while he was still in his prime. The hazard of marrying a woman years older than yourself."

"More to the point – I don't think he ever felt truly loved by Catherine. He knew she would never have married him, had it not been for the fact that Arthur had died, leaving her in limbo, stranded in a foreign country with no means to support herself."

"And that," Elizabeth concludes, "is why Henry has his head turned by romance."

"I don't follow you."

"He never had it, George. His marriage was all about duty."

George stretches like a cat in front of the fire.

"Well I'm all in favour of it. Do you think I would have been appointed Royal Cup Bearer if it hadn't been for Nan? Would father have been reinstated so soon to the Privy Chamber?"

"I'm not complaining..." Elizabeth quickly makes clear. "I just ask myself where it's all going to end."

"She'll have to give in to him," George states as a matter of fact. "Sooner rather than later."

"I can't see that happening."

"Where will we be otherwise? Back at damned Eltham."

He gets up to pour himself more ale. Picking up his tankard, he turns his gaze to the large window on the end wall. And there, on the path through the orchard, Anne is walking along briskly: young, tall, erect, dressed in opulent velvet the colour of emerald green, a rich fur stole wrapped around her shoulders and her hood beset with pearls. Behind her Grandma Butler appears, a comical contrast: bent and gnarled, oblivious to fashion or adornment, covered in layers of drab grey twill.

It is one of those days in late winter that I remember from Hever: the ground wet and muddy, the air raw and chilly, a smell of wet mulch mingling with wood smoke. And, filtering through the overcast sky, the sheer light that is a true harbinger of spring.

"Where do you think you're going?" Grandma Butler calls out to her granddaughter's back, while struggling to catch up with her. "He'll be here any moment!"

Anne hastens her step.

"You have to make him feel welcome!"

Anne walks on doggedly.

"He is the Royal Highness!" Grandma Butler shouts.

Anne stops in her tracks. When she speaks, her voice is firm and deliberate: "I will not end up as Mary. As King Henry's cast-off whore."

Her grandmother flinches. Anne turns to face her.

"All I want is to fall in love again," she says. "Find a man good enough to marry."

"Are you not impressed by the king? Dazzled by his ardour?"

"More like repelled."

"By His majesty?"

"Those piggy eyes...mean lips... mousy teeth..."

Grandma Butler briefly consults her memory. "His teeth aren't bad. Only a few are rotten.."

"His hands and feet are too small for a man his size."

"Now, now," retorts her grandmother. "He has bulk enough where it matters."

"Not according to Mary," Anne quips.

Grandma Butler pulls a face, making them both titter.

Anne sinks down on a bench under a large oak tree. Serious again, she heaves a deep sigh.

"Oh Grandma – I don't know what to do."

Her grandmother sits down beside her, reflects for a while.

"There are occasions in life," she ponders, "when things are best left in higher hands."

"Even if they are quite small?"

They smile at that.

"One skill life has taught me," Grandma Butler continues, "is to embrace the present. Treat it as a gift."

"I've had enough of presents," says Anne, fingering a golden bracelet on her left arm, charms dangling from it, along with a large medallion.

"Fortune favours the brave," her grandmother states emphatically.

"Depends what you mean by fortune."

They get up and walk back to the outer courtyard, where a small boy is playing with a hoop, struggling to get it to roll over the cobbles. His attempts to engage Urian to chase the hoop strike me as faintly familiar. They come to nothing, as the dog is more intent on pursuing a few giddy chickens that have strayed into the yard.

One of them has a lucky escape, when Urian discovers his mistress and rushes up to greet her. Anne pats the large shaggy head, but then the dog turns away, in the direction of the road, and starts barking excitedly. Hoofbeats are heard approaching, enough for grooms to come running from the stable yard.

Anne clasps the shoulder of her grandmother. Her knuckles go white and the old woman winces but does not protest. Seeing the two of them standing there stock still, eyes fixed on the gate house, the little lad drops the hoop and joins them.

A moment later, a group of men ride into the yard. The leader, mounted on a massive grey caparisoned steed, comes to a halt. The grooms and the little boy stare open-mouthed. Urian, too, seems taken aback by at the sight of this awesome creature, larger in stature than any of the other men. He is dressed in a large plumed hat, a doublet of royal blue and a deep red velvet mantle lined with ermine, glistening with jewels catching the soft light of the winter sun. What an impressive sight: His Royal Highness King Henry the Eighth of England, as he was then, at the height of his powers.

He dismounts, and the grooms fold over in deep reverent bows. Anne, whose cheeks have taken on a deeper colour, gives a graceful curtsy, and Grandma Butler somewhat clumsily follows suit, never taking her piercing black eyes off the splendour facing her. Then she remembers the lad, who I now realise is none other than myself. She reaches out a claw-like hand, grabs the back of my little neck and forces it down into a bow. Unprepared, and to the merriment of the entire retinue, I fall flat on my face at the feet of His Majesty. The grooms, too, snigger between them as they lead away the visitors' horses.

I clamber to my feet, looking in terror up towards the king. Equally amused, he pats me on the head, and then does the same to Urian.

Clearly embarrassed, Grandma Butler gives another brief curtsy, then seizes my upper arm to whisk me across the drawbridge, through the gate house under the double portcullis, into the inner courtyard and up the stone stairs to the east wing of the castle. There we join Mary, who, pre-warned, has taken refuge in her bedchamber together with Kitty and young Henry.

Gathered at the lattice window, we all peer out to see Anne and the king talking together down below. Then they head off towards the knot garden, the most private part of the castle grounds, where children are not allowed to play and no servants are admitted. Anne's has to half-run to keep up with the king's giant stride, but once inside the garden he settles down and they begin to wander more sedately back and forth, among knots of herbs that look grey and withered, in abeyance for a change of season, for new growth to come.

The pair stay close together. The king seizes Anne's hand, stopping now and then to kiss it and gaze fondly into her eyes. After a while the two of them disappear into the arbour, out of sight of their spectators.

Mary has been watching this scene in the grip of some powerful sentiment. Tearful, she clutches young Henry to her chest, a sweet memento of the royal favour that was once hers. She has little else left to show for it.

In due course Anne and the king reappear, now in deep discourse. After a long drawn-out farewell, he finally remounts his horse. She waves him off as he rides off ahead of his retinue.

A moment later we hear her come rushing up the stairs. She enters the room, cheeks flaming and the black eyes shining like polished ebony. Her gaze flickers aimlessly round the room before settling on Mary.

Without waiting to catch her breath, she gasps:

"He wants me to be his wife!"

And then she bursts into tears.

"There's no going back now," she sobs.

"There, there," Grandma Butler reassures her soothingly. "Nothing is ever quite as bad, or quite as good, as it appears."

Among the items left to me on my grandfather Thomas' death was a stack of parchment containing assiduously kept records of events taking place from early 1527 up until the cataclysm of May 1536. His elevated position at court combined with his experience as a skilled ambassador enabled him to document accurately and thoroughly the momentous happenings in our country in the context of a wider European backdrop.

This account of his provided me with a reasonably clear intelligence of proceedings in the public, as opposed to the private sphere. I imagine it was written to protect his own name, to establish once and for all that he had played no part in his family's downfall. And while these bare cold facts impress me as being nothing but accurate, I note that my grandfather has been careful to omit any comments of a personal nature. It makes me wonder how much he knew of the whys and wherefores behind these events. Did he know what truly caused them? I ask myself. Who did? Did anyone?

What emerges is that it all emanated from the king's anxiety about the succession. With the Tudor claim to the throne weak and debatable and the threat of rebellion a constant hazard country-wide, His Majesty saw the need for a legitimate male heir as imperative. Added to that, obliquely apparent, was a sense of personal failure brought on by the loss of five royal children, as infants or in the womb. The king feared it placed a slur on his manhood. To make matters worse, his arch rival King Francis kept producing one strapping son after another, by his many mistresses as well as by Queen Claude, even affording his English counterpart the dubitable honour of standing as godfather to one of his princes.

Now, with his consort definitely beyond child-bearing, it was clear that only another queen could secure the Tudor succession. But how would that be possible with Catherine still alive? Henry turned to the Bible, where he presumed answers to most conundrums could be found. And in Leviticus he read exactly what was needed. Verse 20:21 stated clearly:

"And if a man shall take his brother's wife, it is an unclean thing: he hath uncovered his brother's nakedness; they shall be childless."

His Royal Highness had no difficulty mounting massive feelings of guilt and remorse, concluding it was beyond doubt that he had offended the Lord himself by marrying his own brother's widow. Throughout the process, he insisted that this was his sole reason for seeking a divorce from Queen Catherine. A dispensation issued by Pope Julius II at the time overriding the impediment had obviously not been accepted in a higher instance. An action to declare his marriage invalid would therefore be not only necessary but also fully justified.

Convinced that the pope would not hesitate to declare his marriage to Catherine invalid on the grounds of consanguinity and that this would be expedited within a matter of months, the king considered himself at liberty to offer his hand in marriage to the lady of his choice. And once Anne had overcome her reservations and accepted Henry's proposal, she was brought to court from Hever, suitably accommodated in apartments of her own and provided with splendid clothes and jewellery as an indicator of her new status. The whole Boleyn family relished the change in attitude towards them: people who had previously not had the time of day for them were now grovelling and paying homage. A courtier's career depended on being in with the most favoured.

As the king took up the issue of his divorce with Cardinal Wolsey, he found to his relief that his Chancellor was very much in favour of such a move. Wolsey had his eyes set on the French Princess Renée as a suitable candidate for the English throne, and the king did nothing to dispel that illusion. They both realised that, once the king went public with his plans to divorce Queen Catherine, relations with Spain would suffer, as she was the aunt of its ruler, the Holy Roman Emperor Charles V. This was not seen as an impediment: King Henry on his part had had enough of

Charles V's condescending manner towards him, and Wolsey was annoyed with the emperor, who had reneged on plans for a future marriage to the young Princess Mary and defaulted on promised payments to England.

However, it made the need for a new alliance with France paramount. So French support for the royal divorce would be a necessary part of any agreement, and with this objective, a large envoy, headed by the Cardinal and including both father and son Boleyn, was quickly despatched to Paris.

They returned with a group of French ambassadors to celebrate a new Anglo-French treaty in grand style at Greenwich. King Henry, resplendent in a slashed yellow doublet, was on top of the world. For the sake of appearance, Queen Catherine was in attendance at the jousting and seated beside him at the banqueting table, but it was clear to everyone present that King Henry had eyes only for Anne Boleyn, magnificent in apt peacock blue and dripping with pearls and jewels. When the dancing began, it was with her that he opened the floor. To onlookers, this was enough to confirm rumours about the king's impending divorce. Before long, the talk had reached the streets of London, where it caused disapproval, consternation and resentment.

A few days later, a secret ecclesiastical court was convened at Westminster to formally initiate divorce proceedings, but it had to be adjourned, as the matter needed approval from the Holy See in Rome.

With spring passing into early summer, news reached London that unspeakable atrocities had taken place in Rome. The emperor's mutinous troops, numbering some thirty-eight thousand, had pillaged the city and slaughtered most of the Swiss Guard protecting the Vatican, as well as many thousand innocent Roman citizens. Churches and monasteries had been looted and destroyed. And worst of all, as far as King Henry was concerned: Pope Clement VII had been taken prisoner.

This is when the trouble started. Queen Catherine made no secret of her opposition to the divorce, and she had powerful allies. In addition to her nephew the emperor, leading scholars like Bishop John Fisher and Sir Thomas More lent her their support. Wolsey, having discovered to his dismay where the king's true affections lay, tried in vain to dissuade him. But the only concession on His Majesty's part was to send Anne back to Hever, while he went to work on the pope.

First of all, he wrote to Pope Clement VII, asking for a dispensation to marry a woman related in first degree of affinity and who was pre-contracted; the first point obviously referring to his relationship with Anne's sister Mary; the second as a safeguard, should objections ever arise in connection with her romance with Lord Percy, even though both had attested that no such contract ever existed between them. That the sacred rules of the Bible, forbidding intimate relations with more than one member of the same family, applied as much to Anne and Mary as to himself and his brother Arthur did not seem to worry him. King Henry's conscience served him as and when expedient.

He then wrote again to the pope with a direct request to have his marriage to Catherine pronounced annulled on religious grounds by Cardinal Wolsey, making sure the tone of his letter was contrite and remorseful. Towards the end of the year, he had a response: the dispensation requested in respect of Mary Boleyn and Lord Percy had been granted. However, it was worthless, since with it came a statement that Cardinal Wolsey was not authorized to pronounce judgement on the divorce in England. This was an ominous setback, but with the pope still at the mercy of the emperor – what could be expected?

Pope Clement VII was not a brave man. The papacy he had accepted as a sinecure after a tough start in life. He had little interest in politics, or even religion. Now his limited resources of courage had been severely depleted by the depredations he witnessed at the sacking of Rome. In December 1527, he managed to flee to Orvieto, where he felt safer, but he could not risk offending the emperor or his troops. On the other hand, his only protection against a renewed attack by the imperial forces would be France and its ally, England. That meant Pope Clement could not afford to alienate either of them. But how could he condone the English king's divorce from the emperor's aunt without placing himself in an invidious position versus Charles V? Like many people caught between a rock and a hard place, he chose to stay firmly on the fence. Careful not to offend either side, he made an art of pretending to act whilst in effect doing nothing.

Political tension in Europe was running high after the sacking of Rome. The Holy Roman Empire under Charles V had spent years fighting against France over Italy. With France now boosted by an alliance with England, the royal divorce issue became a pawn in the chess game of power between Europe's two main players.

King Francis was prepared to endorse the English king's Great Matter as long as there was something in it for him. The ransom he demanded was military support in his war against the Holy Roman Empire. King Henry saw no option but to agree, even though this was not in his own country's best interests, dependent as England was on flourishing trade with Spain and the Low Countries. The action served to further aggravate his people, who were already taking Queen Catherine's side in opposition to the royal divorce. This added fear of rebellion to the king's woes.

At the English court tensions were also palpable: highly charged responses all round, contrary factions emerging, clandestine meetings, rumours, whispers and secret scheming. All the uncertainty made courtiers loath to declare their hand.

Meanwhile, Anne waited frantically at Hever, her hope for a positive outcome dwindling. But then came the good news: the pope had agreed to send a legate, Cardinal Campeggio, to London to determine the case jointly with Cardinal Wolsey in an English court of law.

To celebrate this long-awaited advancement, Wolsey made a show of inviting King Henry and Anne to a lavish banquet at his magnificent London residence, York Place, where he entertained them with a lavish meal eaten on gold plates and toasts to the pope with the finest wines from Burgundy. Subsequently, Anne and her mother were the king's guests at Windsor. The amorous couple had a brief idyllic spell of hunting together during the day and reading poetry, making music or playing cards at night. They were hopeful once more but wary of taking anything for granted.

The following spring offered no relief. Two eminent theologians, Dr Fox and Dr Gardiner, were sent out to negotiate directly with the pope, but returned home without any definite commitment, other than the promise to send a papal legate. With still no news of Campeggio approaching, tension and suspense mounted once more. Around the country, people were becoming more pronounced in their support for Queen Catherine. With constant rumblings of rebellion, the king was racked by anxiety. Anne, too, was showing signs of becoming increasingly unsettled.

Then at last came the joyful news that the pope had kept his promise: Campeggio was on his way to London! The king and his prospective bride heaved a joint sigh of relief: the legatine court was now mere weeks away. They assumed that the outcome would be in their favour.

Anne settled into newly decorated quarters at Greenwich. Together, she and the king relished the delights of early summer weather: walking in the grounds, boating on the Thames and playing bowls and tennis – that is, Anne watched while the king proudly performed in front of her.

However, the war with Spain was proving disastrous, with heavy losses for the English in terms of both money and lives. It caused deep resentment amongst the common people, who saw no acceptable reason for this war in the first place. The emperor, in a dominant position, exerted pressure on his English counterpart to give up the nonsense of divorcing his aunt. Riots in Kent seemed to suggest the same. And there was no sign of the papal legate appointed to settle the matter once and for all. He had been delayed in France, ostensibly, by an attack of gout.

The lack of progress was intolerable. Anne and His Majesty both fretted. There was nothing they could do but wait and see.

What did come was an outbreak of the sweating sickness: a dreaded mysterious disease, highly contagious and often fatal within hours. People died like flies – in London alone, many thousands perished. It came on suddenly, with violent shivers, giddiness, headache and other pains, and developed quickly into sweat, palpitations, delirium and intense thirst. For those lucky enough to survive, a period of utter exhaustion followed. The Boleyns were lucky to lose only one member of our family and one, it was said, who was dispensable.

The king, terrified of disease at the best of times, had an abject horror of the sickness that had claimed the life of his elder brother. He did what he could to protect himself against this, the worst outbreak so far, by leaving London with a small retinue. At first Anne was with him, but the minute news was brought to him that her maid showed signs of illness, he packed his sweetheart off to Hever. That this put us, her family, at risk of catching the disease obviously did not occur to him.

King Henry only catered to himself. He was the king. He was the one who mattered.

* * *

Looking back, I remember how, in the preceding months, we had seen a lot of Anne at Hever, on and off, arriving unannounced at all times of night or day. But she was not like the Nan we knew. Her temperament was in a constant flux – one day she was elated, dancing around, celebrating some wonderful news she had just received. Then, only a day or so later, having received yet another missive, she descended into the blackest despair, tearing her hair, shouting at us to get out of her sight. Although we children had no idea of the events driving these violent mood changes, it was evident that something of great import was taking place. Even the servants had taken to whispering conspiratorially, cutting themselves off mid- sentence whenever we children entered the kitchen.

I pined for Anne, for my Aunt Nan as she used to be. One late night I thought I heard her arriving, and the following morning I couldn't wait to join her in her bedchamber. Not that I got very far. At the foot of the stairs in the parlour, I was seized by the scruff of my neck by my grandmother. Screaming in pain, I struggled to get away.

"Where do you think you're off to?" she barked, balancing a large pitcher of water in the hand that wasn't grabbing me.

I told her I just wanted to see Nan.

But I was told that I was not to go anywhere near her.

"Why?" I inquired. "Why can't I see her?"

My grandmother then told me that my aunt was very seriously ill. She had been struck down by an illness that had already killed my Uncle William and had nearly cost my father his life. The illness was very contagious. You could catch it, she said, from merely being breathed upon by a sick person.

I was filled with a fear that made my stomach churn. Not for fear of catching the dreaded disease or dying from it. My only concern was for my aunt.

"Is Nan going to die?" I asked tremulously, thinking to myself, if she dies, she will never come back to being herself again.

"I hope to God not," my grandmother replied. "We must all pray for her, as hard as we can. The future of us all depends on her staying alive."

Hever Castle

June 1528.

Hever again. The parlour, looking slightly different from before – I'd say more prosperous. The wall-hangings are of better quality, and there are a couple of paintings, among them a nice portrait of Mary, possibly commissioned by the king for himself when she was in favour and handed over to her father when those days were over. The rushes are fresh, the herbs sweet-smelling. On the table is a bowl filled with flowers from the garden. Outside the window, a mellow afternoon sun can be seen beaming on mature greenery in the orchard.

Mary enters from the entrance hall, dressed in black and carrying a large basket. She places it on the table and looks through the contents. Having found what looks like a letter, she breaks the seal and peers at the writing.

Then Anne appears from the stairs leading to her chamber. Barefoot, wearing only her night shift, she looks dreadful, deathly wan, her hair matted, hanging loose.

"Was that a messenger I heard?" she begins weakly and then adds: "Is that letter for me?"

Mary replies defensively that it came with the basket just delivered.

"And what are you doing with it?" Anne snaps, in a spurt of energy brought on by anger.

She reaches out to snatch the letter from her sister but totters and has to steady herself against the table.

Mary takes a step away from her, clutching the letter.

"This concerns me!"

"It most certainly does not!"

"You promised you would appeal to the king on my behalf."

"Well I did," Anne mumbles.

"And?"

"He did respond. In his letter yesterday."

"And you said nothing to me?"

"For goodness' sake, Mary, I'm hardly back on my feet."

Sinking down in the only upholstered chair, with one hand to her forehead, she holds out her other hand for the letter. Acknowledging defeat, Mary hands it over.

"It's in French anyway."

"I'll read it when I feel better."

Mary unwraps her black travel shawl. The day is hot and sultry, and Anne, panting slightly, is using the letter as a fan.

"Look," says Mary, going up to the basket and picking up a large chunk of meat, "what he's sent you. A whole haunch of venison."

Anne pulls a face of disgust. "Take it away. It's his favourite, not mine."

"You have to try to eat, or you won't get better."

"I could do with a drink."

"Well there's ale here as well."

Mary fills a tumbler and hands it to Anne, who drinks greedily.

"Try some of this. It looks nice and fresh."

She hands her sister a bun. "And this."

It's a lump of cheese. Anne bites into it without much relish.

Mary gives her a moment to chew and swallow and then asks pleadingly:

"Please tell me what he said."

"No."

"No?"

"The king can't possibly be seen to support you. It would give rise to speculation. Imagine the gossip at court..."

"But..." Mary stutters, "William was his loyal servant... a Gentleman of the Privy Chamber, for years and years. I'm entitled to a widow's pension."

"The king says it's for father to look after you and your children."

"Father has made it quite clear that I can expect no help from him."

Anne dismisses this with a wave of her hand. "He can't disobey a royal command."

This does little to relieve Mary's distress.

"It will be on the meanest terms possible."

"At least your children won't starve."

Somewhat restored by the food and drink, Anne straightens up. Having finished her bread and cheese, she empties her beaker and then looks into the basket, finding some plump ripe strawberries. She glances up at her sister, who looks rueful, close to tears.

"Don't worry, Mary," she comforts her sister. "Once I'm queen you can be my lady-in-waiting. I'll give you a good stipend."

"Once you're queen..." Mary repeats, her voice laden with doubt.

"Have a strawberry," says Anne, indicating the basket.

Instead, Mary looks towards the window, which is suddenly obscured by a black cloud outside. A squall can be heard rising, a tremor ruffles the leaves of the fruit trees. Anne, meanwhile, has started reading her letter.

"So what's today's news?" Mary asks lightly.

"Only the usual." Anne gives a feeble smile. "Swearing his undying love. Missing my presence. He begs me to join him without delay, but I'm really not strong enough yet. Life at court has become a nightmare."

"There was a time when you pined for it."

Anne shakes her head.

"All the toing and froing – up and down like a see-saw! The minute I am told that a date can be set for our wedding, someone puts a spoke in the wheel. If not the emperor, the pope. If not his envoy, the bishops. I have no way of knowing who is on my side and who is working against me. No one can be trusted. The slimy prelate least of all."

"Wolsey?"

Anne's eyes turn a shade blacker.

"He exerts far too much influence on the king. One way or other, he'll have to go."

"Be careful, Nan," Mary warns her. "He's a very powerful man."

"I'm in no doubt that it was Wolsey's idea," her sister mutters, "to start this losing battle against Spain. It plays straight into Catherine's hands."

"Well the emperor has to champion her," Mary says. "Blood is thicker than water."

"Worrying about it was enough to make me ill."

Anne picks up a napkin to wipe her forehead. Her hairline looks damp. She then returns to her letter.

"The king," she tells her sister, "intends to stay away from London until the outbreak of sweat is over. He is scared to death of catching it. I keep saying to him that we only get struck down with illness when we can no longer bear to stay healthy. Just as we die, when we can no longer bear to stay alive."

"Like my poor William," Mary sighs.

"They survive," Anne goes on, "who have enough to live for. Like George and myself. The sweat didn't get the better of us."

As the room grows even darker, she continues reading her letter, frowning over it in dismay.

Her sister watches her thoughtfully.

"I don't envy you, Nan," she says. "What you're living through. By comparison, being the king's mistress was pure pleasure."

Anne raises an eyebrow.

Mary smiles. "I just lay back and enjoyed it."

"And where did it get you? To begging your daily bread."

That wipes the smile off Mary's face.

"I play my game differently," Anne reminds her, as she picks another strawberry from the basket.

"I know," says her sister. "But do you think you'll get there?"

"I will." Anne sounds confident. "Whatever it takes, Mary. I'm willing to pay the price."

A flash of lightning suddenly cuts through the room, followed by an instant clap of thunder. Mary goes up to the window and looks out. "This wasn't expected."

"One has to take things as they come," Anne comments calmly. "There's nothing static in either weather or world affairs."

She's looking better now. A bit of colour has returned to her cheeks. Perhaps sustenance was all she needed.

Heavy rain can be heard pattering against the window.

"Tell me one thing, Nan," Mary addresses the deluge outside. "How do you manage to keep his fervour alive without anything to feed it?"

"Oh I feed it all right," Anne smirks. "Little morsels now and then. Not too much, just enough for titillation."

Her sister turns towards her. "And that's enough to satisfy him?"

Anne responds with the mien of a teacher addressing a dim pupil.

"What you fail to realise, Mary, is that nothing impresses the king like virtue. Henry is in awe of my chastity – just as he is in awe of his own."

"Hypocrisy!" Mary scoffs. "It's the way he was brought up! That pious old grandmother of his."

"His conscience is still troubling him over some of the things he and you got up to."

Mary's face softens at the recollection.

"He made no complaint at the time."

"You may have conquered his nether regions – "

"I had his heart too!"

"I suppose," Anne concedes. "His heart and his loins. But I aimed higher than that. I got his heart and his head."

"I'd rather have his loins any day."

"You would, wouldn't you?"

Mary laughs off the implicit disdain.

"What good is a man's head to a woman?

"It tells you what goes on inside it," Anne explains. "It's obvious to me that Henry nurses two obsessions: power and succession. And I hold the key to both."

"What power do you have?"

"I strengthen his resolve. Make him stand firm against the sanctimonious Catherine, the self-willed emperor, the sneering Francis, the odious Wolsey... Against anyone who poses a threat to his sovereignty."

Mary at last, looks impressed.

"As for the succession," Anne continues, "I shall bear him the sons he hankers for. But there must be no question of their legitimacy. That's why we're both agreed that any real intimacy between us must wait until we're legally married."

"I could never do that," her sister declares after a moment's reflection. "When I love a man, I want to do all I can to please him. Give him all that I am capable of."

"Yes, Mary," says Anne wryly. "That's where you and I differ."

She returns to her letter, soon finding something in it that brings a glitter to her eyes.

"He's written me a beautiful new song: '*Adieu Madame et ma Maitresse*'. And he can't wait to sing it to me."

Anne chortles. "He does love the sound of his own voice."

Mary doesn't share her pleasure. Her face is serious, as she sits down on the bench opposite and looks at her sister searchingly.

"Nan – " she asks gently. "Do you love him?"

"Of course," is Anne's blithe reply.

She reads on. The room goes very quiet. The thundery squall has passed.

"Oh yes," she says after a while, looking up. "One thing I forgot to mention. Now, with William dead and gone, Henry has appointed me guardian of your little boy."

"What does that mean?" Mary asks warily.

"That young Henry will be better off as a ward of the Queen of England than as a fatherless commoner."

"So the King has finally come round to recognizing his son." Mary is beaming, her relief obvious.

"Oh no." Anne shakes her head. "He couldn't do that."

"Why not?"

"Think for yourself, Mary. The rules for consanguinity. Admitting paternity to a son of yours would make marriage to me impossible."

Her sister is thinking hard.

"It won't make any real difference, will it? To our life here? Not while my little boy is still so young?"

The king, Anne informs her, wants the boy to be formally educated.

"But not until he's older?"

Mary is trying hard to reassure herself.

"Royal children," Anne points out, "have their own household from the time they are born."

"But my Henry is not royal. He never will be, from what you just said."

Anne makes a point of speaking gently.

"Your son will be brought up in a religious house, specially selected by the king. It's called Syon Abbey and is located not far from London. You may be able to visit him there."

"Not yet, surely?" Mary's anxiety is mounting. "It's far too early for him to leave home."

"Think of the child!" Anne exhorts her. "What's best for him. Try just for once to be unselfish."

Mary gets up and starts walking frantically to and fro. "You'll have to use your influence with the king!" she bursts out.

"I won't let my little Henry leave home until he's old enough to know his mother... Until he has memories to remember me by... I'm the only parent he'll ever have!"

Anne looks at her deploringly.

"Mary – he's already gone."

"What?" her sister cries, aghast.

"They came to collect him. The king's men, to take him to Syon. Earlier on, while you were at Penshurst. I saw them pack up his clothes."

"No!" Mary screams in anguish. "That can't be true! You couldn't have allowed a fatherless two-year-old to be snatched from his mother without even a chance to say good-bye! You would never have done that!"

Anne does her best to comfort her.

"You still have your little Kitty. And young Jojo. He seems to think you're his mother."

Mary pulls her sister to her feet and starts shaking her. "Tell me it isn't true!"

Anne writhes in distress. "Let me go! I'm ill!"

"Say you didn't do it!"

"Leave me alone!"

"Tell me Henry is still upstairs in the nursery!"

"I'm not strong enough for this!"

Mary suddenly lets go of her and rushes off. As her feet pound up the spiral staircase, her voice can be heard shouting desperately:

"Henry! Henry!"

Anne slumps back in her chair, wiping her forehead, catching her breath.

Then she treats herself to another strawberry.

One thing I always regretted was not getting to know my father. Information I garnered over the years confirm my impression of him as handsome, charming and popular; talented, intelligent and well educated. He arrived at court as a page boy aged fifteen and remained close to the Crown throughout his short life. Among his royal appointments were those of Royal Cup Bearer, Squire of the Body, Steward of Beaulieu and Lord Warden of the Cinque Ports. Made English ambassador to France at the tender age of twenty-four, he is said to have got on well with King Francis, helped by his excellent command of French. In the years that followed, he headed a number of significant missions to the King of France.

These facts are all in the public domain. I wish I could have discovered more about his innermost thoughts and feelings. What were his hopes and dreams? His greatest joy, his deepest sorrow? What caused him pain? What touched his heart?

Of particular interest to me is a letter written by him that I found amongst the papers left behind by my grandfather:

"My dearly beloved, Right Honourable Lord and Father," it began. "Please accept my heartfelt congratulations on your double earldom – combining verdant Wiltshire with rugged Ormond. This will keep our Irish cousins in their place for all times to come! Thank you also for allowing me to assume the honorary title of Viscount Rochford. I shall do my very best to honour it for such – hopefully extensive – time as it pleases God Almighty to retain me in my position as your heir apparent.

I look forward with great anticipation to the investiture next month and the ensuing royal banquet at York Place – not to mention the festivities to follow at Hever. That will be a family celebration like none other.

However, much as it grieves me to go against my dear father's wishes, I will not, as you suggest, invite my lady wife to partake in the Hever event. While I accept your point that she, like me, is passing an important milestone, both Jane and myself are in agreement that we are happier apart than together, and her presence at Hever would, in truth, eclipse my own pleasure of the occasion.

I trust, dear Father, that you will respect my deeply felt sentiments in this regard.

Your humble and obedient son and servant,

George."

This letter reaffirms something I always knew: that there was never a trace of affection between my parents. Still – to go as far as excluding his wife from an official family celebration is quite extreme. If nothing else, it was against established custom, which my father was otherwise keen to observe. What could have made him so averse to his wife as to not wanting her anywhere near him? What had she done to deserve such antagonism?

Made an acerbic comment too many, hitting where it hurt most?

I ask myself, as I have done so many times before – why did my parents get married at all? And then, suddenly, the answer presents itself. It is so simple, I can't believe I never thought of it in life.

It was because of me!

Obviously, young Master George Boleyn had got Lord Morley's daughter Jane into trouble, and was made to marry her, against his will and possibly hers, and definitely against the wishes of his parents. Just look at the record of the male Boleyn line: my great-grandfather, having started life as a mercer, managed to snare an earl's daughter for his wife!

And his son, my grandfather Thomas, at the time not even a nobleman, persuaded the granddaughter – soon-to-be the sister – of England's premier duke to join him in matrimony! George, following in the footsteps of this successful line of grooms, would have been expected to bag something like a royal princess. And then, what did he end up with? The daughter of a penniless baron, with nothing better than a pile of old books to recommend him! No wonder Jane was treated with such disdain within this family!

Still – the question remains: why did my father have to marry her? Normally, in a situation like this, the girl would be sent off to the country to live out her pregnancy in obscurity, whereupon the child would be handed over to foster parents so that she could return to court, unsullied, as it were, her reputation intact. Why did the Boleyn family not insist on such a solution, rather than tie these two together in a marriage of little joy or blessing to either of them, and of little benefit to the ambitious Boleyn family?

Trapped in a loveless marriage not of his own choosing, my father might have been expected to settle down, like so many others, with a suitable mistress. Amongst all the courtiers, a man as gallant as himself would have had more to offer than most. Yet no one lady seems to have been deemed worthy of his attention. The only woman he was ever seen spending time with at court was his sister Anne.

I am aware that there has been speculation in regard to his proclivities. Some people – mainly, I imagine, women thwarted by him – were keen to point out that there must have been something deviant with such an attractive man preferring the company of his sister to a tryst with a lover. However, I know exactly where his preferences lay.

Whenever there was a great gathering at Hever, Kitty and I had a straw pallet made up for us in the staircase gallery, so that the room where we usually slept could be used to accommodate prominent overnight guests. Others had to sleep all together in the Council Chamber in the gate house, the oldest part of the castle, which was cold and damp even in summer, with a *guarderobe* open to view. The two of us would be sent off to bed at an early stage of the evening proceedings, and though we were furious to be missing the best part of the festivities, the staircase gallery had one great advantage: a door leading to the minstrel gallery above the Great Hall. So we only pretended to go to sleep like good children and instead sneaked into the gallery. The musicians didn't mind us being there, as long as we didn't distract them or touch their instruments, and they never gave us away.

We hid below the parapet, taking care not to be noticed, peering up just high enough to view proceedings down below. Almost always we found something worth watching, as guests became rowdy and boisterous. The memory that now comes to mind is of the top table: next to my father, a gentleman of ample proportions taking up a fair share of the bench. His costly bejewelled attire, together with his placing above the salt, indicated that he was man of some standing, but however rich and powerful, we found him singularly unappealing where he sprawled on the bench, double chins wobbling.

In his hand he was swinging a tankard that was raised to his lips with alarming frequency. I noticed that my father lost no time filling it up from a silver ewer on the table. In between, the man kept spearing chunks of succulent meat from the trencher placed in front of him, chomping and chewing and talking with his mouth full – table manners that Kitty and I would never have got away with. Worst of all, he started helping himself from an elegant pyramid of gold-dusted sugar plums clearly intended as a table decoration and not meant for eating until it was time for the banquet of sweetmeats.

Beside him was a young, very slender and very pretty woman, also expensively dressed and glittering with jewels. It was difficult to envisage any link between these two extreme specimens of human creation, except that the trencher man kept pawing the young lady in a salacious proprietorial manner suggesting that she was not, as might have been surmised, his granddaughter, but in fact his wife.

They were an excruciatingly ill-matched pair but, with so many marriages based on interests other than mutual love or attraction, this in itself was not unusual.

The husband was quickly losing all signs of reasonable composure, becoming loud and inarticulate. The sugar plums were also taking effect, as he let out a mighty blast of wind resounding all the way up to the gallery. Kitty and I giggled helplessly. Nothing can be more amusing to children than seeing their elders misbehave. Learning this way about the inglorious effects of excessive drinking made it easy for me throughout life to resist that temptation.

The drunkard's pawing of the wife was becoming more intimate – he stretched over his bulging stomach to stick his hand down her cleavage. Embarrassed, she pushed him away forcibly, which was enough for him to lose his balance and topple on to the floor. She stood up, and so did my father. That was when I first noticed a pregnant glance pass between the two of them above the head of her other half. With a combined, not inconsiderable effort they managed to get him to his feet, where he swayed for a moment, fiddling with his prominent codpiece, mumbling something about pissing. My father hurriedly whisked him along to the door, presumably to stop him relieving himself there and then.

After that, the goings-on in the hall seemed tame. Feeling sleepy, Kitty and I snuggled up on our pallet. But just as I was drifting off to sleep, I was alerted by some commotion at the top of the stairs at the far end of the gallery. Peering that way, careful not to show myself awake, I noticed my father and the young lady struggling with her now insensate husband, shoving him towards our bedchamber. They disappeared into the room, and I heard a heavy thud of massive bulk hitting the bed in there – I hoped it wouldn't break under his weight. A brief silence followed, and moments later came the sound of loud snoring.

My father and the wife emerged from the room. He closed the door carefully behind them, glanced up and down the corridor to make sure no one was around – luckily not noticing a nosey child watching, wide awake, as he took the lady in his arms. They kissed for a long time and then continued hand in hand into the bedchamber next door, normally occupied by Mary, who had to share Anne's bed, when my father was in residence.

From this occasion onwards, I never stopped spying on my father whenever there was a gathering at Hever. I believe it was my way of compensating myself for his invariable lack of attention. Mostly I was rewarded by scenes similar to the one I just recollected – many different women, but always young and beautiful, with husbands who compared unfavourably and could easily be persuaded to empty the cups my father kept filling.

It gave me special gratification to know that, despite painstaking measures to maintain discretion, he could not fool me.

As for my mother, I ask myself, how did she fare in this marriage? Did she, like her husband, have an army of secret lovers? I find that hard to envision, having seen no tendency towards warmth or intimacy ever displayed by her. But who knows? She may have had the love of her life tucked away somewhere, an all-consuming passion excluding everyone else from her affections. Perhaps that was why she had so little to spare for her husband and son?

Be that as it may, I still think it was mean to exclude her from the celebration of the family's latest triumph.

Hever Castle

December 1529.

The solar at Hever has also become more opulent. Here it is, decorated with rich hangings, tapestries, paintings... an abundance of candles on the window-sills, carpets instead of rushes on the floor... elegant new furniture... The Boleyn family has been elevated beyond anything that has gone before.

From the hearth issues a sweet smell of herbs burning in the roaring fire, and from the Great Hall come the sounds of a great convivial gathering: minstrels playing, laughter and loud conversation, clatter of silver, bowls and goblets. This may well be the occasion of celebrating my grandfather's two new earldoms.

Suddenly steps are heard approaching up the stairs. The one who enters is none other than my mother Jane, dressed to the teeth to befit her elevation to the peerage. Only her jewellery leaves a little to be desired. She hovers at one end of the room, looking somewhat uncertain. Then there is a sound of more footsteps, and she is joined by her mother-in-law.

My grandmother, too, has gone to some lengths to live up to her new position. Her gown is of sumptuous gold-embroidered silk, adorned with pearls and jewels. Sweeping the floor behind her is a generous trail trimmed with cloth of gold, a fabric allowed only for higher ranks, starting with earls and their wives.

"Oh Jane," she says tersely. "There you are."

Jane bows gracefully.

"Countess."

"I'm so glad," Elizabeth goes on, "that you were able to accept my invitation. It's a long time since we last had the pleasure of seeing you at Hever. "

"Well," Jane replies reasonably, "it's not every day one has cause to celebrate becoming a Viscountess."

"Indeed."

After an awkward pause, Elizabeth pulls herself up to her full height and draws a deep breath, as if preparing to deliver a speech of some significance. Jane looks at her, somewhat guardedly.

"And now," she begins, "time has come for you to switch your allegiance."

Her daughter-in-law looks at her blankly.

"How so, my Lady?"

"You must leave Catherine's household."

Jane gives a nervous flicker of a smile.

"But I'm one of her ladies."

"Not for much longer."

"I've been with the queen," Jane reminds her, "since I was eleven years old."

"All things come to an end," smiles Elizabeth, with enforced patience.

Jane does not share this tone of pleasantry.

"She's been like a mother for me."

Elizabeth remains stiffly amused.

"You're a grown woman, Jane. You have no need of a mother."

"I am to abandon Her Majesty?"

"You have no choice in the matter."

"She has few friends as it is."

Her mother-in-law gives a chilling, unfriendly laugh.

"I should hope so."

Jane remains deadly serious.

"She's been nothing but kind to me. I'm very fond of her."

"Fondness doesn't come into it."

Jane turns away from Elizabeth.

"I came to court as a nobody," she says quietly. "Queen Catherine made me what I am."

Elizabeth loses her veneer of amiability.

"My son, Madam, your marriage to him, made you what you are."

Jane gives her a strange look, impossible to interpret.

"You are now Viscountess Rochford," Elizabeth continues imperiously. "Sister-in-law of the future Queen of England."

Jane seizes on the weakness inherent in this statement. "You're certain of that?"

"As God is my witness."

"There are doubts abroad – "

Her mother-in-law frowns angrily.

"You have had your head turned, keeping the wrong company."

"If you heard what's being said – " Jane suddenly sounds stronger, more confident.

Elizabeth immediately fights back.

"Damn your ears!" she cries. "Have you not eyes to see with? Who was seated next to the king at the royal banquet at Westminster? Where was your precious Catherine? Hiding her face in Greenwich!"

She pauses to check that she has succeeded in deflating her daughter-in-law.

"Make no mistake, Jane," she goes on, calmly and emphatically. "Your place is with Anne."

"You want me to move in with her? At Durham House?"

"The sooner the better."

Jane turns away. There is an ominous pause, before Elizabeth speaks again.

"There is of course an alternative," she says equably. "If you prefer to stay with Catherine."

Jane looks at her, suddenly hopeful.

"You can serve there as our eyes and ears."

"What does that mean?"

"We like to know what goes on in Catherine's household. What she gets up to, who she communicates with."

"You want me to act as your spy?"

"Call it that, if you like."

Jane shakes her head disbelievingly.

"Either that," Elizabeth concludes, "or Durham House."

She stares stonily at her daughter-in-law, until the latter gives a sigh of defeat.

After a moment's silence, Jane asks sombrely:

"What will become of our queen?"

"That's entirely up to her," Elizabeth replies lightly. "If Catherine has any sense, she'll bend her will to that of her lord and master."

"And if she doesn't?"

"You know what happens to those who incur His Majesty's displeasure."

"She is Queen of England..."

"Even Cardinal Wolsey wasn't immune to it," her mother-in-law points out. "Talk about falls from grace. And who, may I ask, is taking over his duties? My very own brother."

Her cold smile returns.

"That's family power for you."

Jane makes a final, brave attempt.

"There are still those who doubt – "

Elizabeth won't have it.

"To hell with your doubts!" she bellows. "Anne Boleyn will be the next Queen of England! And you, Madam, will be her humble servant!"

With that, Jane bows her head.

I am heartened by this view of my mother, showing a touch of humanity, more than I had given her credit for: affection and loyalty towards the unfortunate Queen Catherine. Perhaps Martin Luther was right in saying that there is no person so bad they don't have some good in them.

I also admire her courage to stand up to the hardened stance displayed by my grandmother – a side of her I had hitherto not been aware of. It shows clearly the determination of the Boleyn family to get Anne to the throne. It has been noted that power tends to erode a person's character. I believe the hunger for power has much the same effect.

Wolsey was a casualty on the way. The cardinal had been out of favour ever since the disastrous trial at Blackfriars the previous summer. When, after months and months of delays, it finally started, with the papal legate Campeggio appointed by the pope to determine the validity of King Henry's marriage to Catharine of Aragon, Wolsey had been every bit as confident as Henry and Anne that the court would rule in their favour and annul the existing marriage, thus clearing the way for their nuptials.

At an early stage of the proceedings, King Henry and his entourage were shocked by the unexpected appearance of Queen Catherine. She made a dramatic spectacle of herself, throwing herself on her knees before her husband, vowing that she had been a true, humble and obedient good wife to him and, more seriously, taking God as her judge to confirm that, on her marriage to him, she had been "a true maid, without touch of man", thereby refuting Henry's main argument: that her marriage to his brother Arthur had indeed been consummated, rendering her marriage to himself invalid on grounds of consanguinity.

Adding insult to injury, she had swept out of the hall, proudly and majestically, accompanied by loud cheers and clapping from the large crowd of spectators.

However, Catherine's contribution probably did not affect the case either way, no more than Henry's insincere assertions that his conscience alone had forced him to take this unprecedented step. Neither did the rounds of witnesses and testimonies have any impact. With Pope Clement VII still vulnerable at the hands of the Catherine's nephew the emperor, his legate was never going to rule against her best interests.

For appearance's sake, interminable depositions and legal argument for and against annulment continued up until late July, when Campeggio concluded the hearing by adjourning it indefinitely and referring it to Rome, leaving King Henry and Anne Boleyn as far as ever from the altar.

Someone had to carry the blame for this disaster. Turning his ire on Cardinal Wolsey, the king got parliament to accuse him of having deliberately hampered the progress of the royal divorce. The cardinal was stripped of all his government offices, including that of Lord Chancellor, and made to surrender the Great Seal. In a fearful gesture to appease the king, he handed over York Place, his splendid London residence on the Thames, replete with all the extravagant luxuries he had amassed. The king passed it on to Anne, who lost no time moving in with her family and entourage.

But this wasn't enough. The rest of the chancellor's vast wealth was confiscated. King Henry was particularly keen to lay his hands on Hampton Court, which rivalled his own palaces in grandeur. However, rather than proceed with the criminal charges preferred by Parliament, he allowed the cardinal to retire as Archbishop of York and reside there, in the archbishop's palace.

This was far from satisfactory for the Boleyn faction, who had always regarded the chancellor with suspicion and distrust. They wanted Wolsey out of the reckoning, once and for all. Anne saw to it that the cardinal's overtures to be reinstated came to nothing, and with her family continued to put pressure on the king. He finally relented and had Wolsey arrested – ironically by Lord Henry Percy, whose budding romance with Anne the cardinal had once managed to crush so efficiently. However, by then Wolsey was in poor health. On his way to stand trial in London, he collapsed and died of natural causes.

As King Henry looked desperately for ways to break the stalemate following the failure at Blackfriars, two new talents came to the fore: Thomas Cromwell, who was to prove himself a man of brilliant capacity, and Thomas Cranmer, a Cambridge theologian, who came up with an excellent suggestion: to leave it to European scholars to determine the validity of the royal marriage. Hopeful once more, King Henry had faculties of Divinity across Europe instructed to examine academically the arguments for and against the royal divorce.

In due course, twelve of the sixteen universities approached returned a verdict (with a little help from England's royal coffers) that King Henry VIII's marriage to Catherine of Aragon was null and void. His Majesty managed to get his English nobles and bishops to seal the verdict for despatch to Rome, but it was several months before the pope deigned to respond, and then only by sending a formal order to the king, expressly repeating his prohibition against remarriage without papal consent.

In the meantime, introduced by Anne to the work of William Tyndale, who proclaimed that a king is answerable only to God, His Royal Highness had taken the revolutionary step of declaring himself Supreme Head of the Church of England. The bishops, to avoid economic sanctions shrewdly devised by Cromwell, had no option but to agree. The pope, outraged, ordered the king to appear before him in Rome to answer charges – an insult King Henry chose to ignore.

By reforming the Church of England, the king had cleared the way towards his remarriage, but he still had to contend with widespread unrest at home. The plans for a royal divorce, constantly advocated by the king himself as utterly reasonable and justified, met with disapproval and shows of unstinted support for Queen Catherine, especially from the old nobles. Sir Thomas More, who had succeeded Cardinal Wolsey as Chancellor,

111

resigned in protest. Archbishop Warham of Canterbury likewise sided with the pope, but he at least was old and frail and would not last much longer.

Popular dislike of Anne was so severe and hostility towards her so pronounced, summer progress had to be halted two years running. She was pursued by gossip and intrigue. Particularly damaging were rumours of an attempt to poison Bishop Fisher, a staunch supporter of Queen Catherine. His cook had been told the bishop was in dire need of a laxative and given a medication to add to his food. However, Bishop Fisher was not hungry that day. Not wanting to waste the good food he had prepared, the cook served it up to the bishop's household staff. Two of them died instantly – the rest were said never to be the same again.

Fingers were immediately pointed at Anne as instigator, and the king had to act quickly, attach all blame to the poor innocent, cook, who was punished by being boiled to death in oil – a new effective method dreamt up by His Majesty to discourage murder by poisoning.

With his own health worsening, King Henry was losing patience. In the summer of 1532, having discovered renewed pleas by Queen Catherine for the emperor to come to her aid, he finally banished his wife from court. Orders were given to have her moved to The More in Hertfordshire, one of Wolsey's old palaces. She did not go empty-handed: with her came her household numbering two hundred and fifty.

*   *   *

Though at Hever we were blissfully ignorant of these tumultuous events, we could not help but feel the effect of them. With each arrival of Anne – usually when things went from bad to worse in London and she was ordered to stay out of sight – she brought with her all the tension, anger, anxiety and resentment provoked by circumstances far beyond her control.

"Another delay!" I can hear her shrieking in a voice on the point of breaking, waving in her hand the latest missive from London. "This is no more than a cruel game they're playing! And Henry is allowing it to happen! What kind of king is he? Too weak to stand up for himself, let alone for me! Everyone's turning against me, from courtiers to men and women in the street! I can't show my face without being met by screaming mobs! At court not even my friends are prepared to support me! Catherine's women pleasure themselves baiting me like a cornered rat. And it's all Henry's fault! He's just sitting there like a craven coward, doing damn all to protect me!"

Worse to me was to see her yield to despair, weeping disconsolately over the best years of her life wasted.

"I could have been respectably married by now, to a good man! I could have been blessed with children, I could have been loved and cherished! Instead, my good name and reputation have been taken from me! No one is ever going to want me after this! I will end up a shrivelled old maid, my life poisoned by hatred and enmity that I have done nothing to deserve!"

Kitty and I, with the acuity developed by children left much to their own devices, kept well away from our aunt, accepting that her volatile temper craved plenty of space around her. But one morning Anne came looking for me, suggesting to my surprise and delight that we go and fly her merlin. Only once, a long time before, had I been allowed to watch as she flew her merlin. And it was almost as long since we had last done anything together.

The two of us set off down the path leading to some rough pasture beyond the castle. Anne must have had some good news, for she was for once in her old buoyant mood. It was still early morning, at the beginning of autumn, the sun shone brightly in between tufts of woolly cloud and the air was cool and crisp. In the oak wood over on the other side of the fast-flowing river, trees were on the point of turning, the bracken already a rich russet brown.

Anne carried a shoulder bag and her right hand was covered by a heavy leather gauntlet. Quietly seated on it was Davy, her merlin, hooded and held by jesses. Urian was trotting along behind us, proud and perky as always when engaged in serious work like stalking.

We were planning to get some larks for supper in a spot that was a favourite haunt of theirs. Larks, said Anne, were delicious boiled in milk. Approaching, we stopped for a moment to hear them singing. I felt a bit sad thinking that some of them, unbeknownst, were trilling for the last time.

Hearing them, too, Davy became restless, flapping his wings. Anne took off his hood and released the jesses to let him slip. He flew high up and away, until he appeared only as a small dark speck against a blue patch of sky.

"What if he doesn't come back?" I asked anxiously.

Anne had no such worries.

"He won't let us out of his sight."

Given a sign by his mistress, Urian rushed off to raise a quarry. His shaggy tail could be seen wagging above the tussocks. To begin with, his efforts were unsuccessful and Davy's occasional swoops towards the ground seemed half-hearted, as if he was only warming up. Then suddenly a flock of grey little birds rose from the tall grass. The merlin, from soaring casually high up in the sky, flashed down with the speed of lightning. Before we knew it, a tiny body, limp and lifeless, dangled from his claws.

With a whistle, Anne held out her hand with the gauntlet and Davy landed on it. After courteously handing over the lark, he was rewarded with a chicken foot that he swallowed whole.

She tucked the lark away in her shoulder bag and cast him off again. We watched as he mounted the sky to wait on above Urian, who was working well, ensuring that the birds kept flying. Some of them managed to escape, but for others Davy was too fast and one lark after another was bagged.

Then it was my turn! Anne put the heavy gauntlet on my small hand, added a piece of chicken skin and showed me how to hold out my hand towards the merlin. I had to fight an impulse to withdraw my hand when the large raptor come swooping down upon me, killer claws extended. But he landed very gently on my hand, amazingly light-weight, and willingly delivered yet another appetising succulent lark in return for the unappealing flap of dry chicken skin.

"Why does he do it?" I asked my aunt. "Why does he not eat the larks himself?"

She smiled. "Because I've taught him not to."

How I treasure that memory, the image of her as she was then: carefree and natural, a bit of colour in her cheeks, black eyes glittering in the sun and a soft breeze playing with a lock of her hair that had escaped the hood.

My Aunt Nan as I liked to see her.

As I always sought to remember her.

The Exchequer, Calais

October 1532.

This is a room I haven't seen before. Somehow... different. Not cosy like Hever, not imposing like a royal palace. It is spacious, elegant if somewhat austere, the architecture lofty, with graceful proportions and tall windows cut into thick solid walls. Furnishings are of good quality and so are drapes and hangings, but they give a temporary impression, as if they could be removed at a stroke to leave only plain walls, raw plaster.

And there is Anne, dressed in a glorious gown of black satin, inset with gold-embroidered velvet. She is seated by a sturdy oak table, in front of an ornate gilt mirror. A gleaming coronet takes pride of place on the table and behind her hangs a robe of crimson velvet trimmed with ermine denoting near-royal status.

A servant-girl is receiving some instruction from her. In French. Now I'm beginning to get the picture. When the girl curtsies and leaves with a "Oui, Madame La Marquise", I know exactly where we are.

Calais. Let me see... the autumn of 1532. And most likely, we are in the Exchequer, the administrative headquarters built by the English following their conquest of this territory.

Now alone, Anne unlocks a casket in front of her on the table. She opens it and starts pulling out a dazzling array of jewellery: emeralds, rubies, pearls... adorning herself with one piece after another: rings, pendants, brooches...necklaces, bracelets, headpieces... a gold pomander beset with sapphires... until she is totally laden.

When the door opens, she gives a guilty start but, relieved at the sight of her sister, goes back to admiring herself in the glass.

Mary, wrapped in a fur-lined cloak, is standing still by the door, animated like I've never seen her before: breathing rapidly as if she's been running, her cheeks flushed, eyes shining with a dreamy, faraway look.

Anne smiles at her reflection.

"If only Catherine could see me now! I bet these look better on me than they ever did on her."

Mary takes none of this in.

"How foolish of her," Anne goes on, "to make such a fuss. What good are the crown jewels to her where she is now? She knew I'd get them in the end."

She starts putting the jewellery back into the casket, keeping only a plain strand of pearls.

Mary takes off her cloak.

"I can't believe what just happened," she murmurs.

"Did you find him?" her sister asks sharply.

"You know the soldier downstairs?" Mary goes on absently. "Guarding our entrance. Tall, blond, handsome – "

"Have you got it?"

After hesitating a moment, like someone coming to from a dream, Mary opens a drawstring velvet bag and pulls out a rolled-up parchment. She hands it to Anne, who takes it over to a window-seat, where the light is better.

"Did he suspect anything?"

"Suspect?" Mary is still distant.

"Who it relates to?"

"Oh? No, not at all. I said it was for my husband."

Satisfied, Anne starts studying the parchment.

"What he said was..."

Anne makes no reply. She is too busy reading.

"He said, he'd been watching me on board the Swallow. He was hoping I'd get seasick, so he could come to my aid..."

She gives an inward smile.

"I'm glad I didn't."

Her sister is absorbed by whatever is on the parchment.

"And he couldn't believe his luck when detailed to guard our quarters at night. I told him I shall sleep very well knowing he is there watching over us. To which he replied: 'Rest assured, Lady Mary, I'd lay down my life for you.'"

"Is this all?" says Anne, referring to her document.

"No one has ever said that to me before."

"Said what?"

"That he'd lay down his life for me."

"The astrologer said that?"

"No. The soldier. At the door."

"You've been parleying with *a soldier?*"

Mary makes no reply.

Anne is shaking her head.

"Really, Mary, you're out of your mind. You are now the sister of the Marquess of Pembroke. We don't talk to *soldiers.*"

Her sister turns away.

"Don't ever repeat such folly."

Over at the other window, Mary is looking out, craning her neck.

"Now listen to this," says Anne. "I'll translate for you: 'His sun sign is Cancer'... We all know that...'Not the grandest of signs, needs good strong aspects to mitigate a tendency to pettiness'..."

She chuckles. "He wouldn't like to hear that.... 'A square to the Moon means he didn't get to choose his position in life, but favourable Moon aspects from Mercury and Saturn make him a good leader'... That's true... 'Mercury at a sinister angle to Saturn indicates a lack of paternal support, resulting in poor self-esteem'...Hmm... 'Virgo rising projects him as chaste and virtuous'... I have noticed... 'A nice sextile from the love planet Venus makes for ease in expressing his feelings'... Oh yes, indeed!... 'However, Gemini is an unfortunate place for Venus – makes him fickle, destined for multiple partners'... We'll soon put a stop to that... 'Furthermore, Venus' conjunction with his Mid Heaven square his Ascendant suggests ignominy linked to his love life'... Oh well... 'Main problem in this chart is the warrior planet Mars. Badly afflicted by Jupiter, it leads inexorably to poor judgement, rash decisions, disastrous consequences.'"

Anne throws down the parchment.

"Is this all?" she asks, and when there is no reply from Mary, continues: "It's not what I expected. Did you not tell him I want to know what the future holds?"

Her sister turns back from the window and whatever held her interest there.

"He wouldn't go into predictions. According to him, that's not what astrology is for."

"Then what does he think it's for?"

"To show the hand you've been dealt. How you play your cards, he said, is up to yourself."

As Anne contemplates this, Mary throws another glance towards the window.

"I wouldn't mind having my fortune told," she says wistfully.

"Why? Your fortune is but an adjunct of mine."

Anne gets up, throws the parchment on the fire blazing in the beautifully carved stone hearth.

"What a waste of money. He didn't say a thing I didn't know already."

* * *

The two sisters are now standing in a gallery overlooking a vast hall. Down below, scores of servants are busy preparing it for a spectacular reception: on either side, rows of windows are draped in cloth of alternative gold and silver; heavy logs are piled into huge fireplaces at each end of the room. Trestle tables are being covered with crimson damask, decorated with gilt candelabra and gold centrepieces brimming with pearls and jewels. Shelves stacked with gold plate are rigged up along the walls where passages are left clear for processions.

"Is his new queen coming with him?" Mary asks innocently.

Anne's eyes take on a deeper shade of black.

"Have you not heard? She and her miserable French dames made a show of their disloyalty by refusing to receive me or be received by me. Even my old friend Marguerite of Angouleme."

Mary gives a little grunt of sympathy.

"If only Queen Claude had been alive... Anyway, that is why Henry had to go all the way into French territory unaccompanied by me. And why Francis is coming back with an all-male following. He threatened to bring Duchess de Vendome along, but that's when I put my foot down."

"Why? What's wrong with her?"

"I will not have a royal mistress present at my court."

This brings a furtive smile to Mary's face.

"As a matter of fact, it will be an advantage to have Francis here all alone. It will be easier to get him to agree."

"Agree to what?"

"Support for our marriage. Why else do you think we're here?"

Anne goes on to describe her plans for the evening. Francis will be given a time he'll never forget. First there will be entertainment for the two kings and their respective retinues, numbering a couple of hundred people. An array of superb delicacies and the best French wines will be ceremoniously presented, till the two of them can manage no more. Meanwhile, the two sisters and four other selected ladies will be dining privately in a separate chamber.

This seems to disappoint Mary but Anne continues unperturbed. Once the tables are cleared and the minstrels start playing, the six ladies will make a spectacular entrance, wearing elaborate costumes and masks specially fashioned for the purpose. She herself will invite the French king to open the dancing with her and only after he's danced himself dizzy, will King Henry intervene to unmask her and so reveal her identity. After that it will be for Anne to withdraw with Francis to a quiet corner, where they will devote themselves to some very serious conversation, aimed to end in a pledge for his unswerving loyalty.

"Oh Nan, I wish you luck."

Smiling conspiratorially, Anne leads her sister down a corridor. She throws a door open to reveal another room: a huge bed chamber, occupied by a giant four-poster, the oak bedhead elaborately carved with Tudor roses. It has hangings of bright green trimmed with gold, a counterpane of gold and green brocade and a pile of soft cushions swathed in cloth of gold; two tall windows either side of the bed are draped with the same fabric. The walls are bedecked with rich tapestries, the floor with oriental rugs in blazing colours. On a table a massive silver candleholder set with at least a score wax candles is waiting to be lit.

"I've had this specially prepared for Henry," Anne tells her sister.

Mary stares, impressed.

"As splendid as anything he has at home."

"It is for a very special occasion," Anne goes on to say, lowering her voice confidentially. "You see, I agree with the astrologer. About playing your cards with the hand you've been dealt."

Mary looks at her inquiringly.

"I have decided to play my trump card."

Anne then reveals that this night, after the banquet, she will surrender herself to the king, here in this bed. Time has come to force his hand — no more dilly-dallying. After that Henry will have to marry her, to ensure that his heir is legitimate.

"If you get pregnant, you mean?"

Anne raises an eyebrow at the absurdity of this question.

"I have every intention of getting pregnant!"

"But how can Henry marry you without the pope's permission?"

Her sister gives her a look full of forbearance.

"Henry is now the Supreme Head of the Church of England! He doesn't need anyone's permission!"

Anne leads her astounded sister on to another room nearby: another bed chamber, every bit as splendid as the former, only in different colours: crimson, sapphire blue and silver, and with *fleurs-de-lys* instead of Tudor roses as adornments.

"This is where Francis will retire once he's had enough of dancing."

"He'll approve of these comforts."

"And so will you," Anne sniggers.

Mary shows no response.

"You know better than most how to please a man."

Seeing no assent forthcoming, she adds:

"It's the least we can do to reward him."

Only now does Mary realize what is being asked of her.

"Nan – I couldn't do that."

"Why not? You've been with Francis before."

"When I was thirteen years old. A virgin."

"Well I daresay you'll get more out of it more this time round."

"I won't do it, Nan."

Anne goes in to sit on a chest at the foot of the bed. Having given herself a moment or two to compose herself, she begins to explain, as patiently as she can, the political situation: never her sister's strength. England, she declares, is in a very precarious situation, surrounded by powerful enemies. The pope and the emperor have overcome their differences and decided to join forces, no doubt urged on by Henry's open defiance. At first it was thought this might be an advantage: their father had been sent out to Bologna to negotiate with the two of them jointly, but returned saying he might as well have stayed at home and hit his head against a brick wall. The king accused him of having made matters worse.

"Just imagine," Anne goes on, "what will happen when news of our marriage leaks out. The emperor, in league with the pope, is bound to take action against us to avenge his aunt."

Mary is not overly concerned. Brother George has told her that, even though the emperor's military might is considerable, England has little to worry about. The imperial forces have their hands full fighting the Ottomans on the eastern flanks of his territory.

Anne knows better.

"Charles has just won a resounding victory over the Turks. His army is already heading west. The only thing to protect England against a Spanish invasion will be an alliance with France."

Mary shrugs it off.

"Francis has always been your friend, hasn't he?"

"Not anymore," Anne mutters darkly.

"Why? What's gone wrong?"

"One thing after another. The King of France has agreed, after decades of hostilities, to a peace treaty with the emperor, setting the two of them up against England. On top of that, Francis, still with his eye on Italy, has betrothed his son Prince Henri to Catherine de Medici."

Seeing her sister's lack of response, Anne fills her in:

"A member of the richest, most influential dynasty in Florence."

"Is she not even royal?"

"Worse than that, Mary."

"Worse?"

"She's the pope's niece."

Mary turns again to the tall window. She stands there for a while, looking out searchingly.

"So you do realise," her sister addresses her back, "that we need to do all we can to please Francis?"

Mary turns to her, shaking her head, her eyes filled with tears.

Anne's black eyes flash angrily.

"Don't you understand what's at stake? The future of our country!"

"I can't do it, Nan. I couldn't."

Sobbing, she rushes from the room.

Not overly disheartened, Anne goes up to straighten a fold in the counterpane. She expects to have her way. Mary is but a card in the hand she's playing.

These glimpses into the past, gathered from private intimate exchanges behind closed doors, are providing me with fresh insights. But how come they are conveyed almost exclusively by women? Where are the men? Have they nothing to contribute?

"They have already had their say," I hear a voice behind me.

Swivelling round, I discover my grandmother Elizabeth coming towards me: poised, in command as always.

"History," she goes on, "as we all know, is written by men, for men and about men, listing actual, incontrovertible facts. But there is another side to each story: the women's experience, doomed to for ever elude posterity. Two versions of the same historical process: one objective, the other subjective."

"So which is more valid?" I ask. "Where do you find the truth? Halfway between the two?"

She replies, more likely by encompassing both.

That leads me to another question: "Are you saying that men and women approach life differently?"

My grandmother hesitates briefly. "I can only judge by my own observations."

"So let's hear."

She gazes into the distance, gathering her thoughts. I wait patiently until she begins, and then stay very still and quiet, so as not to distract her.

"Of my three children, Anne was the one I had the highest hopes for. She was bright and level-headed from an early age and with her sunny disposition a joy to have around. In 1512, when my husband returned from a diplomatic mission to the Netherlands, bringing back a generous offer from Archduchess Margaret of Austria to receive our elder daughter into her household, we both agreed that Mary, at the age of twelve, was too immature for such a challenge. Anne would be more suitable: though over a year younger, she was clever and well-mannered and fluent in French – unlike Mary, who had no ear for languages. And so it was that, aged ten and a half, Anne left her home and travelled to Mechelen, to become a member of an illustrious European royal household.

"I was confident," my grandmother continues, "that she would be well able to look after herself. And the reports we received from Mechelen were highly favourable. The archduchess even wrote personally to thank us for letting her have the pleasure of Anne's company! The following year, when both our daughters were selected to form part of Princess Mary Tudor's retinue on her marriage to King Louis XII of France, we felt Anne would be a good support for her older but less experienced sister.

"After the wedding, King Louis dismissed most of the English attendants, but a few maids of honour were allowed to stay, among them our two girls. We were glad to see them settled at the splendid French court. But then, only three months after his marriage, the decrepit French king died – some say, due to his exertions in the bed chamber, while others, more prosaically, blame gout.

"The young Dowager Queen of France soon remarried her paramour Charles Brandon, Duke of Suffolk, and returned with him to England. Our elder daughter, in hindsight unwisely, was left to fend for herself at the court in Paris, while Anne, already a favourite of the devout Queen Claude, was brought to live with her in the palace at Blois, a far safer place for a young girl. And there she stayed until looming war between France and England made it necessary to bring her back to England."

Elizabeth's eyes narrow as she debates how best to continue.

"Anne wasn't long home by the time she encountered the young Lord Percy. The two of them fell head over heels in love, and they were both heart-broken when their romance was stopped. All that remained for my daughter was to aim for another love like it – only this time, for someone she'd be able to marry. Nothing else would do. That's why she remained impervious to the king's one-sided infatuation."

She rolls her eyes.

"Her lack of response only served to fuel his ardour, the way an elusive prey encourages a keen hunter. And there was more to it. The discovery that the object of his pursuit was chaste, virtuous and honourable was to him proof that she possessed exactly the qualities that had been lacking in her sister. It constituted a reassurance that, with her, his affections had found a safe haven.

"For months on end he persisted, without gaining much ground. Then, at some point, it must have occurred to him that Anne could provide him with more than a love interest. If he made her his wife, she could also bear him the legitimate heir he craved. And once Anne realised what she stood to gain, she had no difficulty finding in her heart enough affection to keep Henry spellbound.

"To begin with it looked so promising. 'He loves me, Mother,' she'd confide venerably, her eyes brimming with tears. 'And I adore him. Just imagine all the good we will be able to accomplish once we are king and queen. England will thrive under our reign.'"

The memory brings a sad smile to Elizabeth's handsome face.

"Still, Anne had her doubts. Following the king's proposal and her own formal acceptance, she sent him a brooch depicting a lady in a storm-tossed sea, confirming that she was under no illusion that her way to the throne of England would be plain sailing. But the king assured her that the only stumbling block was a mere formality: his marriage to Catherine was about to be annulled, leaving the two of them free to marry in the near future. Neither of them had any inkling of the massive wall of obstacles they were about to encounter, once the king's plans for divorce began to seep out."

Looking into the distance, Elizabeth frowns.

"Anne was strong, clever and morally impeccable. She had so much to offer the world. And yet... I was astounded to see the vitriol levelled against my poor innocent daughter, not only at court, but country-wide. As early as that first summer, when His Majesty took her with him on progress, letting her ride beside him, while the queen and her ladies were relegated to the back... People along the road spat and cursed after Anne, calling her a whore. And she wasn't even the king's mistress! My presence as chaperone did little to protect her reputation."

Annoyance is beginning to seep into her voice.

"You would have expected the people of England to take to their hearts one of their own rather than a foreign princess, who did not even speak their language properly. But not at all! Seeing no further than their noses, they regarded Catherine as a lawfully wedded wife, Anne as an impostor threatening the sanctity of marriage, on which most of them, especially women, depended.

"Anne herself, basking in the glory of her new position and the king's public displays of affection, was content to let it pass. Accepting the king's argument that his divorce and remarriage were not only justified, but an absolute necessity to secure the survival of the Tudor dynasty, she saw her role as essential to her country's future. She was not going to have her equilibrium rocked by the rudeness of a few peasants along the way.

"In the months that followed, little was achieved. The pope made a practice of giving with one hand and taking away with the other. Meanwhile appearances at court had to be observed. The first Christmas was formally celebrated by the king and queen at Greenwich, pretending all was well, while Anne was told to stay quietly with her family at Hever."

With an involuntary shiver a dismal holiday is recalled:

"Nothing but low spirits and misgivings! The weather as cold as any of us had ever experienced. Both the well and the moat were deep frozen so that ice had to be brought from the river and melted to provide water for the household. Only the kitchen could be heated to a tolerable level and we huddled there, together with the servants. At night we had to sleep with the dogs to keep warm.

"We struggled to keep our spirits up, clung to the hope that our wretched seclusion was all in a good cause, trusting that by next Christmas, probably much sooner, all would be resolved. Little did we surmise that this was only the beginning of a pattern set to continue for years: an interminable succession of progress followed by setbacks, all induced by circumstances far beyond our control – indeed, beyond anyone's control. We were caught in the middle of it, like rabbits in a snare."

She heaves a deep sigh.

"Ignoring the fierce resistance: from his queen, from the emperor, from the pope and, not least, from the majority of his English subjects, King Henry persevered in his efforts to obtain a divorce. Having started this battle, he had no option but to see it through. His Royal Highness was not one for accepting defeat, as anyone could testify who had seen him tilting, thrusting himself all out at his opponent with no fear of injuries to himself or anyone else. Here his honour was at stake. He had no intention of going down in history as a loser.

"Drawn in as combatants on his side were myself and your grandfather, your parents and your Aunt Mary, my brother Norfolk and his family and many others. We were all beset by the same determination to overcome the opposition. In my view, King Henry wasn't driven by love for Anne, nor by a lascivious desire to physically possess her, as many assumed. His obsession was with winning, and Anne constituted his shimmering, tantalising prize trophy. As for her well-being – he simply did not care.

"My poor girl became a hostage in the game raging over her head. She must have suffered more than any of us realised. Her temper flared more readily, her way with words made her tongue ever sharper. Increasingly overbearing as a form of defence, she managed to turn even her allies away. Not even His Majesty was safe from her furious allegations: of misleading her, ruining her life, annihilating her good name and honour, exposing her to plots and intrigue.

"Hearing her verbal attacks, I was horrified. His Royal Highness did not take kindly to being challenged – his response to such liberty could be ruthless. But faced with Anne's fury I saw him crumple, break down in tears, plead with her, do all he could to appease her. That usually meant showering her – even the rest of her family – with extravagant gifts and favours. It didn't help her cause: as Anne moved around the city in a splendour to rival the king himself, she only made herself even more unpopular."

Elizabeth shakes her head dismally.

"Like any mother seeing her child become the object of undeserved malice, I longed to come to her aid. Protect her against hatred and intrigue, desolation and despair. But all my position permitted was to stand by, powerless.

"And then one day, the battle was over. A new chapter began. By exceptional means never envisaged, Henry emerged victorious. On January the twenty-fifth, 1533, I was present to see my younger daughter, pregnant by the King of England, become his wife and queen.

"I'm sad to say, it brought me none of the pride a queen mother would be expected to feel. All I could think of was the Nan I had once known and loved: a sweet, beguiling young girl, full of life and love for the world. Looking at the royal bride, what I witnessed was the toll taken by seven long years of turmoil and uncertainty, of suspense and broken hopes, of hatred and hostility. And I realised that a terrible price had been exacted.

"My heart felt as heavy as lead, and deep inside me an ominous voice whispered: *This will not end well...*"

Tower of London

May 1533.

No longer at Hever, but in a place of much greater splendour – newly built, by the looks of it. Walls are gleamingly white-washed, hung with glorious tapestries, silver brocade and cloth of gold. The room is dominated by a throne raised on a platform, the benches along the walls are upholstered in damask. Oh, now I know! We are in the Tower of London, the queen's apartments, erected for Anne in time for her coronation.

And there is my mother Jane, sprawling on the throne, most definitely not a seat intended for her. She is decked out in a sumptuous gown of purple silk, with a matching hood and a huge amethyst pendant. Over by the large mullioned window is Mary. Funny how she is often found like that: standing by a window looking out, like someone incarcerated longing to escape. She, too, is beautifully dressed, in light blue damask, with an expensive-looking sapphire necklace.

The window is opened wide, bright sunshine streaming into the room. Lush foliage outside suggests a day in late spring. There are sounds of a crowd nearby, a cannonade being fired, trumpets blown.

"Here they come!" cries Mary. "Hundreds of boats, following in the wake of the queen's barge!"

"The noise is giving me a headache." Jane clutches her ears.

"My dear little sister," Mary muses fondly, "arriving like the Queen of Sheba."

Her sister-in-law remains caustic.

"She's lucky the barge wasn't sunk by Catherine's supporters."

"It belongs to her now," Mary reminds her. "She's had Catherine's initials removed and replaced with her own. Three times as large!"

She looks out again.

"She's stepping ashore. The king is there, waiting to receive her."

A cheer is heard from the crowd.

"What was that racket for?" Jane wonders.

"He put his hands on her belly and kissed her with great reverence."

"Oh don't make me puke."

"It was really sweet."

Her sister-in-law takes a different view.

"The way those two are showing off... You'd think they're the first pair in history to have managed the feat of conception."

"Well it is the heir to the throne," Mary avows.

"Only if it happens to be a boy."

"It is a boy! Everyone says so – doctors, astrologers, sooth-sayers..."

"Because it's what the king wants to hear. I'll believe it when I see it."

Mary looks out again.

"She's walking up the path... Beaming from head to toe. A living image of her own motto."

"What did she settle for in the end?"

"The Most Happy."

"The Most Happy?" Jane scoffs. "That is the most ridiculous motto I've ever heard in my life.

"It's how she feels."

"A royal motto," her sister-in-law goes on, "should express something to commend you. Like *Honesty Above All* or *God's Will My Duty*. Not be used as a licence to wallow in your own good fortune."

Mary jumps to the defence of her sister.

"She just wants to share her happiness..."

"Share? With whom? She no longer has a thought for anyone but herself. Don't tell me you haven't noticed.

"Well..." Mary concedes. "I did try to tell her what happened to me in Calais... But she wasn't interested."

"Exactly," says Jane. "You and I have been reduced to a pair of buttresses with no other function than to prop her up."

"At least we're included as an essential part of her new life."

"Yes," her sister-in-law agrees. "Because we are the only ones who put up with her airs and graces. You and me and George and your mother."

"Even father's patience is wearing thin," Mary says, half amused.

"Someone ought to inform Anne what being ro yal is all about. Serving your people, not using them for your own glorification."

"Let's hope it's a passing phase."

"It's time she stopped pandering to her own needs and wants," Jane mutters. "Her main concern should be to create a favourable impression."

A rare note of bitterness enters Mary's voice.

"She could take a few lessons from the king. All he cares about is the impression he makes."

"Even in bed?"

"Particularly in bed," she titters.

At this point footsteps are heard approaching. Jane quickly jumps up from the throne and hovers politely nearby.

The door opens, and Anne comes sweeping in: magnificent in a gown and train of yellow satin with sleeves of cloth of gold. A gold brocade bodice laced over her bulging stomach gives a fair display of her swelling bosom, and her large pieces of jewellery are set with pearls and topaz. The overall impression is of glorious radiance, as if the sun itself had burst into the room. Except this sun does little to illuminate: it renders the other two pallid, eclipsed, instantly outshone.

"Did you see the reception I got?" she beams. "Did you hear the cheering?"

"Indeed." Jane sounds anything but enthusiastic.

"Wasn't it lovely," Anne goes on, her eyes glittering, "the way he put his hands on my belly?

"Yes, delightful!" Mary smiles benignly.

139

Anne makes herself comfortable on the throne.

"The look in his eyes. So tender..."

She falls silent, dwelling contentedly on her triumph.

Mary and Jane exchange glances, aware no doubt that, with Anne's new status, they are not supposed to speak until addressed by her.

And it isn't long before the queen turns to them with some practical concerns.

"Well my ladies..." she announces formally. "I have a few minutes before dinner. So let's run through the arrangements for Saturday's procession to Westminster. You'll be pleased to hear that the two of you will play a prominent role throughout my coronation."

Jane and Mary bow graciously in reply.

"Lady Rochford – you come and sit here on the floor on my right – "

Jane stares at her. Anne looks back.

"With you," says Jane, "I'm always Jane."

"Not any more. Jane is not a suitable name for the queen's sister-in-law. You are henceforth to be known under your formal name, Lady Rochford."

"If you say so."

"That's no way to address your queen!"

"I beg your pardon, Your Majesty."

"That's more like it. Now you sit here on my right, and you, Lady Mary, on my left."

Jane and Mary sit down on the dais on either side of her.

"If she can be Lady Mary," says Jane, "why can't I be Lady Jane?"

Anne gives her a scathing look.

"Really, Lady Rochford – have you learnt nothing during your years at court? Lady Mary is the daughter of an Earl. You are merely the wife of a viscount."

Jane makes no reply.

"Is that clear?" Anne asks acidly.

"Yes, Your Grace."

There is a pause. Mary glances towards her sister, anxious, it seems, to be in her good books.

Anne informs them that for the procession they will both be in crimson velvet, riding with five other ladies in two chariots painted red and gold, following immediately behind herself and the Lord Chamberlain.

"Will you be in a chariot, too?" asks Jane.

Anne smiles condescendingly.

"I shall be in an open litter resting on two palfreys caparisoned in white damask, with golden plumes, under a canopy of cloth of gold carried by the Knights of the Cinque Ports."

"What will you be wearing, Nan?" Mary inquires politely, only to get a furious response.

"Don't you dare call me Nan! Never again! I am your queen."

"Sorry, Your Majesty."

"I shall wear a surcoat and mantle in white trimmed with royal ermine. My hair will be hanging loose, from a coif of jewelled circlet. And my slippers will be of gilt leather."

"So you're leading the procession?"

"My dear Lady Mary, what would that be like? A queen leading a procession? First will come twelve Frenchmen, on horseback.

"Frenchmen?" Jane sounds surprised.

"A gesture to please dear Francis. To thank him for his support."

"Dear Francis," mumbles Mary, deadpan.

Anne takes no notice. After them, she continues, will come gentlemen, knights and judges, in robes, on foot. Then the Knights of the Bath in their purple gowns, followed by abbots, bishops and the peers of the realm – all wearing crimson velvet.

"Just like us," says Mary.

"Except they mightn't be in gowns," puts in Jane.

Anne keeps ignoring them. Next, she says, will come the Lord Chancellor with the Archbishop, Lord Mayor and Ambassadors, all in ceremonial dress. After them it's for herself to appear, with her train of court ladies in chariots, plus some fifty more ladies and gentlewomen on foot. The King's Guard will bring up the rear, followed by lackeys and archers.

"Some procession," Jane concludes.

Anne nods indulgently.

"What about tomorrow?" asks Mary. "What's happening then?"

Anne tells them that the whole day will be spent preparing the processional route. Streets will be strewn with gravel, hung with tapestries, carpets, silk and velvet. To the sound of church bells pealing, all the guilds will be lined up along the road, and the squares will have pageants with allegorical figures proclaiming poetry in her honour.

As she draws breath, Mary looks thoughtfully at her sister.

"And how do you think the people of London will take to this spectacle?"

"They'll love it! The fountains will be flowing with wine...

"And the streets of vomit..." Jane is quick to fill in.

Anne scowls at her.

Jane has more to say.

"If you don't mind, Your Highness... Might I suggest that perhaps it would be prudent not to appear overly exultant?"

"Lady Rochford!" Anne exclaims. "What on earth are you saying?"

"Well," Jane goes on, quite undaunted. "You know what the populace are like... They might appreciate a glimpse of something they've seen before..."

"Like what?" Anne's voice is as sharp as a razor.

"A modicum of modesty, perhaps."

Her queen stares at her, incredulous.

"I think she's got a point," Mary agrees. "It might not be a bad idea to temper all that pomp and glory with just a sprinkling of humility."

Anne's black eyes are shooting sparks.

"Humility?" she cries. "Have you two forgotten what I've had to live through? Seven years of endless humiliation! My pure and honourable liaison with the king dismissed as a sordid affair! The emperor and his sorry vassal the pope branding me as a "concubine" – no better than a whore – just to humour that obstinate cow Catherine! Then the moth-eaten wreck Campeggio stringing us along, building up our hopes, whilst all the time knowing full well that his so-called trial was nothing but a cruel, long drawn-out sham."

Passion brings her to her feet, as she continues:

"And then I lived to see my own English people – about to become my subjects – take Catherine's side against me! Pursue me with catcalls and abuse, set out to physically attack me! On two occasions I had to run for my life! Be ignominiously rescued by boat from a mob baying for my blood!

"Even at court I'm surrounded by nothing but menace – hatred, jealousy and envy – enemies wherever I look! You talk to me about humility! You ought to hang your heads in shame!"

"Your Majesty – " Jane, scrambling to her feet, makes an attempt to placate her. "I'm sure Lady Mary was only speaking in your own interest."

"I'll tell you what's in my interest!" Anne roars. "To tolerate no more humiliation! To have my enemies tracked down and punished!"

She glares at the two of them.

Mary, too gets up.

"Just one small thing," she ventures very gently, "that perhaps you ought to be aware of..."

"What?"

"You know your and the king's initials... H and A put together. Signs of them going up all over London..."

"What about them?" Anne's voice is as cutting as ever.

Mary tempers it by making hers nice and soft.

"It has been suggested that they could invite mockery. You know, as in HA! HA!"

Anne's black eyes glisten ominously.

"Let anyone try to mock us! We'll have them arrested for treason and they won't mock anyone ever again!"

She makes a dignified effort to compose herself.

"Now – the king is expecting me to dine with him..."

Majestically, as befits a queen, she marches out.

Mary and Jane look at her departing figure, then glance at each other.

A Field by the Thames

June 1533.

The scene has changed once more. We're in a field by a river, presumably the Thames, for further downstream, under a deep blue sky dotted with fluffy white clouds, the outline of many houses and smoke from chimneys can be espied. Judging by the lush grass, the surrounding fresh greenery and a delicate scent of roses, it is early summer. A maypole is still standing, but the garlands dangling from the cross pole look sad and withered, no longer inviting anyone to dance.

This would be a Sunday or possibly St Erasmus' Day, for the field is teeming with people out to enjoy the good weather: families, couples and groups of youngsters, eating and drinking, laughing, playing, having a good time. With the prohibition against gatherings within the city walls, residents of London soon got into the habit of seeking out pleasant meadows within easy reach, in which to enjoy their pastime.

For no particular reason, I notice one particular family, who have made themselves comfortable on a threadbare piece of matting. Three sweet little children are being fed in turn by a rotund mother, while the father, a rough-looking character, looks with pleasure at his offspring, sitting patiently like fledglings, their mouths open in anticipation of the next morsel to be plucked from a large basket.

The idyllic scene makes me smile. But my pleasure quickly turns to concern when I notice the object resting behind him on the threadbare mat.

A lute.

Having helped himself to some food out of the basket and swigged lustily from a jug, the man gets to his feet, picks up the lute and moves over to an open patch of grass. Striking an ill-tuned chord, he instantly attracts the attention of those present. They form a close circle around him, looking as expectant as any fledgling: eager, open-mouthed.

The vain hope I'm nursing that we are going to hear a pleasant little ditty in praise of love or summer is crushed when I hear the ruffian address the crowd.

"Good day, innit?" he begins. "And better still it'll be when ye hear what I have to sing. For I know what ye're all thinkin'. That ye're afeared of sayin' out loud. But I have no such fears. I'll sing fer ye all. I sing for the people of London."

Met with loud cheers, he strums the lute and sings:

> "A hateful harlot has seized the crown;
> To power she is prone.
> She chased Queen Catherine out of town
> And robbed her of her throne.
> Although the King has made her queen,
> We don't accept the switch.
> It won't be long before he's seen
> He's married to a witch."

Inviting the bystanders to join in the chorus, he doesn't have to ask twice:

> "HA! HA! HA! HA! HA! HA! HA!"
> they all sing joyously.
> "HA! HA! HA! HA! HA! HA! HA!"

The self-appointed balladeer takes off his dirty woollen hat and places it upside down on the ground. Coins are dropped and thrown into it, as he continues with a second verse:

> "The hateful harlot likes her gold
> And pearls and jewels fine.
> But Londoners will not be fooled:
> She's not of royal line.
> Although the King has made her queen,

We don't accept the switch.
It won't be long before he's seen
He's married to a witch."

Once more they all take to singing. I notice the women being particularly zealous:

"HA! HA! HA! HA! HA! HA! HA!
HA! HA! HA! HA! HA! HA! HA!"

More coins hit the woolly hat.

Is no one aware that this is a very dangerous game? And am I the only one to have detected a hint of movement behind a thicket of wild roses and brambles at the edge of the field?

The balladeer goes on:

"The hateful harlot will soon depart,
She won't maintain her sway.
She'll lose her place in the royal heart.
He'll send her on her way.
Although the King has made her queen,
We don't accept the switch.
It won't be long before he's seen
He's married to a witch."

"HA! HA! HA! HA! HA! HA! HA!"
bellow the chorus.
"HA! HA! HA! HA! HA! HA! HA!"

Meanwhile, I have been keeping my eye on the thicket. And I wasn't mistaken. Two royal guards, armed with pikes, suddenly break their cover. The crowd are so busy lustily haha-ing they don't notice. Only the lute-player's wife does. Giving a loud scream, she starts running with her children. Her husband,

149

throwing down the lute, is not late to follow, and the next moment everyone is on the move, darting in all directions.

The balladeer is the one they are after, the one they pursue. He is not the fittest of men and they soon catch up with him, grab him and march him off to a barge anchored by a jetty a bit further off.

The wife, watching, is in tears. The children, too young to appreciate what is happening, start bawling in sympathy. She walks past left-behind remnants of food and drink, playing cards and children's toys, up to where the lute was abandoned. Treaded on by many feet, its wood is now splintered, the strings broken. The woolly hat is likewise trampled, the coins it contained scattered. Sobbing, she collects as many as she can find, then picks up the hat and the ruined lute and walks off, her little ones trailing behind her.

I shudder at the thought of the fate likely to befall her husband.

The more I see, the more I feel that I am being drawn inexorably towards some form of a conclusion, although it may still be a long way off. The process reminds me of arrangements at court, where attendants start out in an open watching chamber admitting them all; only some are privileged enough to advance gradually through presence and privy chambers, the aim being to reach the ultimate goal: the bed and stool, mind and heart, of His Majesty himself.

I started out with information accessible to all and sundry, but as I discover more and more, it brings me ever closer, not to the king, but to my own loved ones. Might it end in the full comprehension of all that became their life and mine? A state where no further progress is possible?

A pattern is indeed beginning to emerge: like the warp set for a tapestry. And it is for me to weave it together into an intelligible whole, using as weft my own observations, reflections and... what else? I suppose, memories. Without memories no life tapestry will ever be complete.

Like the late summer following Queen Anne's coronation. At Hever, Kitty and myself, Grandma Butler and the household staff, were all on tenterhooks awaiting news of the queen's confinement. Her lying-in at Greenwich was being attended by her mother, sister and sister-in-law, as well as other prominent ladies of the court.

We were more than a week into September by the time our grandmother made an appearance. Kitty and I stood lined up with the servants in the inner courtyard to welcome her home, but she ignored us, just walked straight past and on up the stairs towards her own private bedchamber.

The austere look on her face gave rise to wild speculation amongst the servants. The child must have been stillborn! Or worse still, Queen Anne might have died. Perhaps they were both dead!

It was more than Kitty and I could endure. After deliberating between ourselves, we made our way up the stone stairs to see our grandmother, though unsure whether we'd be admitted.

We found the door open, herself still in her travel clothes, sitting in an easy-chair, preparing to do some embroidery – something she often resorted to when discomfited.

"Is Nan dead?" I called abruptly from the doorway, unable to contain myself.

She looked up from the needle she was in the process of threading. "Of course not," she said absently.

"Is it the baby?" Kitty filled in. "Did the baby die?"

Elizabeth let her hands rest on her lap, then took a deep breath. "Anne and the baby are both doing well."

We waited while she started her stitching: a chair cover depicting the Boleyn coat of arms: something she'd been working on for some time.

"It's a girl," she muttered.

"B… but…" I stammered, "we were told she was having a boy."

"That's what everyone expected," she said. "Especially His Majesty."

She started sewing again, stabbing the needle angrily through the cloth, adding stitch to stitch to a background of royal blue.

"What's wrong with it being a girl?" Kitty demanded – bravely, I thought.

Our grandmother sighed. "The country needs an heir."

"Can't a girl be an heir?" my cousin persisted.

At that Elizabeth gave a shrill yelp, having pricked her finger on the needle.

"Get out of here!" she ordered us. "I need peace to get on with my sewing!"

We went downstairs, through the gatehouse, into the outer courtyard. It was a murky sort of day, dark clouds swollen to the point of bursting into a heavy autumn rain. Urian came to meet us, wagging his tail, and we took him for a walk in the herb garden, defying the ban on children and dogs there. We were too preoccupied to stop the dog cocking his leg over thyme and sage destined for the kitchen.

"I can't see what's wrong with it being a girl," Kitty reiterated, this time to me. "Girls are as good as boys."

"Not really," I told her. "Boys can do things girls can't."

"Well so can girls!" was her rejoinder. "Girls can do things boys could never manage. Not in a million years!"

"Like what?" I said, my unbroken voice already rife with the disdain of unquestioned male superiority.

"Have babies!" Kitty cried triumphantly.

Annoyingly, I had no answer to that.

In the evening the following day, our grandfather arrived at Hever. He told his wife that, like her, he had considered it politic to get out of His Majesty's way. The king was raging and venting his fury on anyone coming close.

Though only the four of us, we had dinner in the Great Hall, at one end of the large table. No servants were admitted, as our grandparents were intent on discussing this latest misfortune. They behaved as if Kitty and I weren't there, but then, we were used to being ignored and, in any case, much of what they said went above our heads.

"Anne will have to change her ways," our grandfather declared. "Being high and mighty with her own is one thing, but the king will not suffer it."

"She has changed since becoming queen," Elizabeth reflected.

"Queen or not, she is his subject and must behave accordingly. The way she lays into him! You heard it yourself, only the other day."

Our grandmother instantly took her daughter's side. "That was because of his flirtation with that silly girl. He should never have – "

"His Majesty is answerable to no one!" her husband interrupted her. "And he's made that clear to her, in no uncertain terms."

"My daughter will never accept adultery," our grandmother stated proudly.

"She'll have to from now on. Her position – as well as ours – has been greatly compromised by the arrival of this accursed child."

"I'm sure sons will follow," his wife mumbled.

"That's no comfort to the king! After waiting seven years, after breaking with Rome, antagonising the Emperor, risking foreign invasion, turning his own people against him... All for the sake of giving the country a male heir – and now this!"

"At least the little girl is strong and healthy," our grandmother pointed out.

"What good is that? She's not even first in the line of succession. Catherine's odious daughter has primogeniture."

"But if the king's first marriage is declared invalid, Mary can't inherit. Then Anne's daughter becomes heir to the throne."

Her husband gave a loud snort. "There's no way she could ever be Queen of England."

"Why not?" This was Kitty piping up.

Our grandfather turned towards her, staring as if only now he had become aware of her presence. "What do you mean, child?" he growled.

"Well Aunt Nan is Queen of England, so why can't her daughter be the same?"

This met with a disparaging look. "Anne is queen because she married the king. That's completely different."

"In what way?"

"A woman couldn't rule the country."

"Why not?"

I was holding my breath in secret admiration of my cousin's courage in challenging our grandfather this way. But he didn't fly into a rage. He threw back his head and laughed heartily.

"A woman on the throne of England!" he guffawed. "Chairing the Privy Council, leading an army into war, quelling rebellions? Now that's a sight I hope I shall never live to see!".

He didn't live to see it. Neither did his wife.

But Kitty and I did.

*　*　*

Notwithstanding the king's disenchantment, appearances had to be maintained. Documents prepared in advance to announce the royal birth hastily had the letters 'ss' added to the word 'prince' and the baby was christened Elizabeth after her two grandmothers. The occasion was celebrated with due pomp and circumstance, my father playing a prominent role holding the canopy over the little princess as she was carried forth to the font.

But in private, the king's main obsession showed no sign of abating. It was understandable – with the constant threat of a Spanish invasion and rumblings of rebellion nationwide, he desperately needed a male heir to strengthen his tenuous hold on the throne. In the event of his dying with no legitimate successor in place, his country would be laid open to both civil war and foreign conquest. Perhaps that was the main reason why Spain had opposed his divorce.

England's relationship with the great powers of Europe reached a nadir when, after Princess Elizabeth's birth, Pope Clement VII took the offensive step of officially declaring King Henry VIII's marriage to Catherine of Aragon legal and valid. This made England's schism with Rome final and irrevocable, King Henry liable to excommunication. His instant response was to get Parliament to pass an Act of Succession making his issue with

Anne Boleyn, regardless of gender, rightful heirs, thereby refuting any future claim to the throne by Mary Tudor, his daughter by Catherine.

Princess Mary, or the Lady Mary, as she was now styled, was proving herself to be a formidable opponent, in fact much more dangerous than her mother, who had settled at Buckden Towers with few comforts and a greatly reduced household, devoting her time to feeding the poor, sewing altar-cloths, praying and doing penance wearing a hair shirt. King Henry's attempts to derogate his daughter by stripping her of her royal title and moving her from Beaulieu Palace into little Princess Elizabeth's household at Hatfield had met with stubborn opposition. Boosted by support from the pope, her cousin the emperor and, alarmingly, by a considerable portion of the English populace, she persisted in styling herself Princess Mary and referring to her stepmother as a whore.

The emperor himself, Charles V, was keeping ominously quiet. Perhaps he was biding his time, waiting to see how long the English king's infatuation with his new lady would persist? His emissary, Eustache Chapuys, had spent years doing all he could to denigrate Anne Boleyn. In order to preserve necessary diplomatic relations, the liability for the royal divorce was laid firmly at the door of Anne and her family, branding them all arch enemies of the emperor and his kin.

As for King Francis, he remained on ominously good terms with Charles V, and the marriage of his second son Henry to Catherine de Medici, the pope's kinswoman, had gone ahead as planned, strengthening France's foothold in Italy.

Duly concerned, King Henry resolved to pay a personal visit to his old friend and ally across the water. However, his plans for travelling had to be put on hold, as Queen Anne, he was pleased to announce, was again pregnant and so would be unable to rule the country in his absence. Perhaps he was also aware that his queen, pregnant or not, would have been left dangerously exposed as regent on her own.

Hostility against her was more intense than ever. The crown's brutal measures to enforce the Act of Succession had turned the country into a tyranny. Esteemed churchmen, devout bishops, priests and monks, were being incarcerated for refusing to accept the king's second marriage and his adjunct break with Rome. Many were executed – hung, drawn and quartered – on charges of treason.

Thomas Cromwell, as Principal Secretary the second most powerful man in the country, carried the responsibility for both reform and terror. On his initiative, the first moves were made towards a dissolution of the monasteries, on grounds crassly material rather than religious. The royal coffers had been depleted by pointless, ruinous warfare, and now the huge wealth amassed by the monasteries beckoned welcome relief to the Treasury.

Neither the king nor Cromwell appreciated the degree of displeasure this would invoke among the common people of England, who loved the unattainable splendour of their abbeys, found comfort in their looming presence, enjoyed the celebration of countless holy days. Reducing the might of the monasteries meant depriving English villagers of a relished constituent of their daily life.

Again, the one who was given the blame for it all was none other than our Nan who, perhaps unwisely, had made no secret of the fact that she'd been committed to the New Religion ever since her early days in France. The stamp of heretical impostor clung to her, and all the country's woes, from shortage of food caused by trade impediments, to increased taxes to fund the war, were seen as a result of her interference in public affairs.

Even the king, always keen to blame someone else for his own mistakes, was beginning to take the view that his wife was at fault.

These were dark days for Anne. With her matrimonial relationship deteriorating and court support in short supply, she turned increasingly to her own religion, spending her days in prayer, pleading for a healthy boy-child as fervently as Catherine of Aragon had done before her. Like her predecessor, she would have been well aware that only the birth of an heir to the throne would secure her position and regain her husband's devotion.

Whitehall Palace

September 1534.

This, I gather from the imposing architecture, has to be a royal palace. From the sight and sound of traffic on the river outside the handsome bay window, it is probably Whitehall, once Cardinal Wolsey's York Place, now in the process of being substantially rebuilt and extended. The lack of attendants suggests that we're in a private chamber.

In spite of the grandeur of this room, it looks untidy, uncared for, as if interest in it is waning... Furniture is placed haphazardly, a shawl is thrown casually over a throne-like chair; books and other personal items are scattered willy-nilly.

No one is present – no, I take that back, in the darkest corner a woman is kneeling on a prie-dieu, lost to the world in abject prayer. I am all in favour of religious devotion, but still... something about this prone figure is not uplifting.

And now my Aunt Mary enters the room. She, too, makes an uneasy impression. She is not herself, not Mary as I've been used to seeing her. Though looking lovely as ever, there is something evasive, even furtive, about her. She is carrying a garment of sorts, clutching it to her front. Looking around guardedly, she stops to watch the dejected figure in the corner. Getting no reaction, she asks gently:

"What's that you're so busy praying for?"

The Queen of England, for it is she, lifts her head and looks at her, then sighs and straightens herself up, in a conscious effort to pull herself together.

"Oh Mary," she says disparagingly. "Have you've learnt nothing of the New Religion?"

Mary looks uncertain.

As countless times before, Anne starts lecturing her older sister, explaining to her that we are not supposed to 'pray for things'.

"God is not an old man sitting on a cloud handing out sweetmeats when we ask for them."

Her sister looks even more puzzled.

Anne gets to her feet.

"You pray to get closer to God. To find the strength of spirit to make his will your own."

Mary frowns, reflecting.

"Then how do you know if your prayers are answered?"

Anne's reply is slow and deliberate.

"When your prayers don't bring the desired results, it means, not that God has failed to listen, but that you have not listened to Him."

It makes little sense to Mary.

"I still prefer Mass in Latin."

"Like so many," Anne sighs. "Taking the easy way out."

Mary's eyes flicker around the room in search of some diversion. Settling on a book lying open on a table, she goes up to peer at it more closely. I get the feeling that she wants to avoid getting too close to her sister. The book, as it happens, is one of Anne's prayer books, an unapproved English version. Mary turns the pages without much attention. She has never shown any great interest in either books or religion.

"Where have you been?" Anne sounds reproachful. "I haven't seen you for weeks."

Immediately defensive, Mary reminds her that she did send a message that she'd stayed behind in Greenwich. Because she wasn't well.

"That was last month."

"Yes."

"What's wrong with you?"

"Oh – " Mary hesitates for a moment. "A stomach complaint."

"Will I send for Doctor Butts?"

Doctor Butts was the answer to any ailment at court. I'm not sure I would have entrusted my health to him, but the king swore by his medical skills and that was enough for the rest of them.

Mary reassures her that there is no need. She is better now. And I must say, she has the look of someone in excellent health – she is positively blooming.

Anne sits down on the throne-like chair, staring morosely ahead.

"You mustn't stay away like that, Mary," she says. "Even if you're not well."

In response to a marked difference of tone in her voice, Mary glances towards her.

"I need you here," Anne impresses upon her. "With George away in France, you and Jane are all I have."

"And Mother," her sister hastens to add.

Anne shakes her head. "Father won't let her near me anymore. He's set himself up against me."

"Why? What have you done?"

"I have done nothing!" Anne retorts. "It's he who can't accept the fact that he has to defer to me. He complains that I don't show him 'due respect'. That I treat him like a dog."

She snorts. "Same with Uncle Norfolk. These men – they have been grumbling for years. Unable to come to terms with a woman above them in rank."

"Especially if she's their daughter or niece."

Anne is suddenly tearful.

"They've turned the whole court against me. At a time when I really need my family's loyalty and support."

Drawing closer, Mary contemplates her sister with a look of sympathy that makes her more like our Mary of old.

"I heard you lost your baby," she says very softly.

Tears are rolling down Anne's face.

"Henry has been vile to me ever since. It's like he wants to punish me for failing him – again."

All of a sudden Mary is full of compassion. The life-long intimacy between these two sisters, missing a moment ago, has returned.

"It was bad enough to give birth to a daughter," Anne weeps.

Mary does her best to comfort her.

"That's very unfair."

"Have you noticed, Mary," Anne says, in an effort to control her tears, "how Henry has changed? He's no longer like he used to be."

Her sister nods sombrely.

"Nothing like the man I once knew."

They both fall silent, thinking, perhaps, about King Henry, as he was and how he has become.

Then, seemingly inconsequentially at first, Anne starts to talk about Davy, the merlin she had at Hever. Hawking birds, she expounds to Mary, who never flew a hawk in her life, form a strong attachment to their handler. Simply because you supply them with something they relish: succulent morsels of their favourite meat. In return they do your bidding: bring back the quarry you're after.

Mary's only response is that she doesn't like birds of prey. Their beady eyes make her uneasy.

Anne goes on to convey her view that this is what love is all about: we form an attachment to someone who can supply what we want. Henry wanted a son, she herself wanted the crown.

"Well," says Mary not unreasonably, "so far you are the one who got what you aimed for."

"But it's a crown of thorns, Mary, bringing me more pain than pleasure."

She sighs despairingly.

"What I find is... if you don't fulfil your part of the deal... that is, if you can't provide the reward... that's the end of the attachment. The bird flies away."

"But that's not love," says Mary.

"It's the only form I know."

"Is that what you had with Percy?"

"Oh don't remind me of Percy!" Anne exclaims. "I'm doing my best to forget him!"

I can see Mary searching for the right words to state her case.

"Well then think of your little dog: Purkoy. His love for you knew no conditions. It didn't lessen if you forgot to feed him or chastised him when he misbehaved."

The memory makes Anne's tears flow anew.

"Dear little Purkoy. Killed by my enemies, just to torment me."

It is a while before she speaks again.

She wants to know, has her sister heard the latest gossip? Mary says no, she's been away, that is, she immediately corrects herself, she's been ill. Anne pays no attention. Preoccupied, she goes on to disclose that Henry made an attempt to seduce one of her attendants – a young girl, just up from the country.

Which one? Mary inquires, but Anne replies, never mind, she's gone anyway. Gone where? asks her sister. Back, says Anne, to wherever she came from.

"The little slut. I got Jane to deal with her."

"The right person!" chuckles Mary.

Her sister the queen makes it clear that she will not tolerate any immorality in her household. It's bad enough to have an invidious stepdaughter and her crowd doing all they can to denigrate her. She intends to show the world that they are wrong about her. That she is every bit as worthy and devout as Catherine considers herself.

"If not more so," Mary humours her.

"Catherine is of the old school," Anne goes on. "She believes the mumbling of endless prayers and mortification of the flesh confer sainthood. I'm a step ahead. The New Religion puts the onus on faith and conscience, on love of righteousness rather than fear of divine retribution."

Mary's face takes on the blank look she always wears when theology enters the agenda.

"I do more for charity than Catherine ever did!" Anne declares proudly. "Forty smocks I sent to the poor house only this week!"

This is language Mary understands.

"I made three myself," she tells her sister eagerly. "This one is just finished."

And she holds out the smock she's been clutching to her front all this time.

Anne snatches it from her, and Mary quickly turns away, as if something the other side of the room has suddenly attracted her attention.

Her sister instantly recognizes that something is wrong.

"Don't turn your back on me!" she commands, suddenly all regal. "Show me your face!"

Mary slowly turns around. Anne stares, incredulous, at her bulging stomach. A long silence follows, during which Mary keeps her eyes fixed submissively on the floor.

"A stomach complaint?" Anne pronounces grimly.

Mary peers up at her.

"I'm sorry, Nan. I didn't know how to tell you."

In return she is awarded a look of utter disgust and condemnation.

"You've gone back to your old wanton ways! Here at my court! Disgracing us all – "

"It's not like that – " Mary protests feebly.

"What in Heaven is God thinking," cries Anne, "taking my baby away, whilst letting your whoring bear fruit?"

She stares at Mary, suddenly horrified.

"It's not Henry, is it? Oh, do tell me it's not him!"

Her distress has a calming effect on her sister.

"No, Nan," she replies. "It's not Henry. It's my lawfully wedded husband. I'm a married woman once more."

Anne says she can't be. As the queen's sister, she can't marry without permission from the king and herself. Mary tells her she wouldn't have given it. Why? Anne asks sharply. Who is he?

Mary smiles.

"A commoner. William Stafford. He was in the king's retinue at Calais."

"A common soldier?" Anne exclaims, outraged. "And you considered yourself too good for the King of France!"

"William was the man of my choice."

"And you succumbed to him," Anne mutters in disgust, "like the whore you are! The whore you've always been!"

Mary straightens up and meets her eye, no longer timid or submissive.

"You've got it wrong, Nan," she says equably. "Whores are the ones who sell themselves for money – or for rewards, like birds of prey. Like yourself, as you've just established."

Anne is speechless, shocked at the turn this conversation has taken.

Mary continues, undaunted:

"I gave myself to William because I love him and, strange as it may seem, he loves me – as I am, with all my flaws and failings. Not that you would understand – the closest you've ever come to love is what you got from your lapdog."

"You seem to have forgotten," her sister gasps, "that you are talking to your queen."

Her words do not impress Mary.

"Your position, Nan, makes no difference to me anymore. I don't need you or anything you can offer. What I have with William is all I require. All I shall ever want."

Anne's eyes, blacker than ever, could cut through ice.

"When the King hears of this," she growls, "you'll never set foot at court again."

"I have no wish to," Mary informs her. "I've had no life here as your servant – picking up the crumbs from under your table. Playing my part in your contrived efforts to appear superior to us all."

The Queen of England looks totally at a loss. And her sister isn't yet finished.

"I tell you, I'd rather starve and beg my bread with William than share another day of your miserable life!"

"You will starve!" Anne proclaims. "I will see to it that you do!"

Even this threat doesn't deter Mary.

"William will see to it that I don't. He has inherited a little farm in the country. It will provide just enough for us to get by."

The queen has had enough.

"Get out of here, Mary!" she shouts. "Get out of my sight! I never want to set eyes on you again."

Mary goes calmly towards the door, but before she exits, turns round.

"Good-bye, little sister," she says. "May God be kind to you. Kinder than he has been so far."

Anne slumps on the throne, her desultory figure incongruous with these splendid surroundings. She is no longer tearful, only furious, but that doesn't make her any less pitiful.

She looks terribly, heart-wrenchingly lonely.

Mercifully, she is joined by my mother Jane.

"I heard your raised voices," she says, "and thought the better of intruding. What on earth is going on?"

"Don't ask," is all Anne can muster.

Seeing the state her queen is in, Jane hesitates briefly, but then she has to divulge that she is bringing some bad news. Can't be worse than the news I just had, is Anne's response.

Jane tells her she was summonsed by Cromwell.

"That pestilent meddler!" Anne sneers, "what did he want?"

Her sister-in-law tells her that she has been banished from court. She has to be out before sunset. Anne dismisses this as nonsense. Cromwell has no authority to interfere with a member of the queen's household.

Actually, Jane says, he was acting on the king's order. This has Anne instantly on guard. She has been banished by the king? Yes, says her sister-in-law, he's found out about the girl.

"The little slut from the country?"

Jane nods. "She'd written to him complaining that I'd sent her packing."

"I hope you told Cromwell it was due to her slovenly ways?"

"Yes, Your Grace. As you suggested."

Anne is thinking hard, seriously concerned.

"Did he realise that you were acting on my instructions?"

"He didn't ask," says Jane, after a moment's hesitation.

"Was anything said that could affect the king's disposition towards me?

"No, not a word about you. All his ire is directed towards me."

"Oh good."

Jane begs Anne to speak to the king, put in a word for her, but she replies she couldn't possibly.

Her sister-in-law pleads with her:

"I need your help, Majesty. You are the only one the king will listen to."

But her queen informs her that this is too delicate a matter.

"If Henry gets an inkling that I was behind it, he'll take it out on me."

"I don't want to leave court!" Jane exclaims.

"He'll have the girl brought straight back – just to spite me."

"But where will I go? I have no other home!"

"There's Beaulieu."

"George's doesn't want me there."

"So go to your mother in Norfolk."

"I shall be so miserable."

Anne makes an attempt to console her:

"Henry's tempers don't last for long. You need to stay only a short while. Till he gets over it."

"Till another lady takes his fancy."

"No Jane – " says Anne. "I'll win him back. I shall have to."

As her sister-in-law looks doubtful, she continues:

"Henry needs a son, and I'm the only one in a position to bear him a legitimate heir. He knows it, too. We are chained to each other, by circumstances forged in iron. We have no option but to see this through."

A silence follows.

"I'd better go and pack my belongings..." Jane says eventually.

"But – " Anne exclaims, "What about me? How shall I manage without you? With Mary gone as well... I shall be all alone, surrounded by enemies – like a lamb left to a pack of wolves! Oh, don't leave me, Jane! Please stay!"

"I can't disobey the king."

Anne is in tears once more.

"Promise me you'll come back soon."

Jane is equally moved. "As soon as ever possible."

They embrace, whereupon she leaves.

Again, Anne is alone.

As I grew up, I accepted that both my parents were committed to life at court, rather than to their offspring. But there was one occasion, on an early summer's day in 1535, when my father finally took an interest in me. How proud I was to hear that he had travelled to Hever specially for my sake.

At this time, around thirty years old, he was at the apogee of his career. I remember him clearly: beautifully dressed in a red damask doublet, striped hose, a velvet mantle in black and gold, fashionably slashed sleeves and a hat with a broad white plume.

Leading the way upstairs to the long gallery on the second floor, he told me this room, extending from one end of the castle to the other and measuring no less than a hundred feet, had been added by his own father for his wife, who found Hever as it was then lacking in grandeur. The gallery was where we took exercise or played on rainy days, and where much socialising took place, with music and dancing.

My father looked happy and comfortable as we settled, just he and myself together, by the large mullioned window at the west end, where mellow rays of the evening sun filtered in. Chatting amicably, he told me he had just come back after yet another mission to France. The French king had come up with a proposal for his eldest son, the *dauphin*, to marry Princess Mary, or the Lady Mary, as she was now styled. This was seen by our King Henry as a clear affront. Acknowledging his eldest daughter as a royal princess, suitable as consort to the future king of France, was the same as accepting the pope's claim that his first marriage to Catherine of Aragon had been legal and valid.

His Majesty had been mortified to learn that, if he repudiated the proposed match, aimed to forge an amicable link between their two countries, an alternative marriage would be arranged between the *dauphin* and the emperor's daughter. This would create an all-powerful European alliance that would leave England precariously isolated and open to a joint invasion.

To counteract implications inferred by the proposed match between the *dauphin* and the Lady Mary, my father had then been charged with the task of persuading the French king to agree to a second future marriage, between his third son and little Princess Elizabeth. To begin with, King Francis had responded positively, but then he requested an exorbitant sum as dowry for the princess. This was another insult! As far as King Henry was concerned, his French counterpart should think himself favoured by this generous offer of an English princess of royal blood as consort to his third – third! – son!

My father informed me that while, regrettably, he had returned with his mission unaccomplished, he had every intention to persevere. He fully agreed with His Majesty that maintaining the long-standing friendship with King Francis was imperative, especially since it had come to light that Cromwell was not averse to a new alliance with the emperor – he was even said to be making secret overtures in that direction. Such a policy would spell disaster for the Boleyn family, hated adversaries of Charles V.

Aged only ten, I was thrilled to note that he was talking to me as to an adult, though now I realise that this was probably not because he regarded me as one but more because he had scant experience of dealing with children.

He went on to tell me that Kitty would soon be going off to London to join the queen's household.

"Yes, Sir," I replied, "so I gather. I shall miss her company. It makes me wonder, what's to become of me?"

"Well," my father replied good-humouredly, "I hear you're making good progress in your study of the New Religion."

Eager to please him, I hastened to rattle off a summary of the tenets our latest tutor had impressed on Kitty and myself: that salvation came, not from indulgencies, not from confession and penance, but from faith alone, and that everyone should have access to Scripture in their own language and commune with God directly, with no need for intermediaries, like priests or saints.

"Very good," my father mused approvingly, making my heart race with pleasure. "The time is ripe for a new approach to religion. Everyone must be given a chance to find their own faith and discover for themselves what it means to be a true Christian."

To this I could but nod my agreement.

"For that," he went on, "they will need good decent men to guide them along the way. I have decided that you will be one of those."

He lost me there. I looked at him blankly, while I tried to work out what this meant.

My father smiled benignly, making me feel that, whatever he came up with, I would happily go to the end of the world to fulfil his expectation.

He told me that, within a few days, I was to be despatched to a college of priests in Suffolk. The dean, Mr Matthew Parker, was a kinsman of my mother, and he would take a personal interest in my education. Like most of my family, he was fervently committed to reforming the church.

I could feel my mouth agape.

"I will be a priest?"

"It will give your life value and purpose."

My father got up. I followed his gaze as it fell on the fruit-trees below: white blossom tinged rosy in the glow of the setting sun. After a while he turned back to me.

"What I wish, my son," he said gently, "is for you to bring some good into the world."

And then he added gravely, half to himself:

"God knows it's needed."

* * *

I never saw my father again. So I never had a chance to thank him for giving me the greatest gift of all: the joy of scholarship. And for sending me to Stoke-by-Clare: a sacred place of learning, where I immediately felt at home.

Almost a year I had – not even a year – of blissful innocence... Until the fateful day in May 1536, when Mr Parker himself interrupted a lesson in Divinity, calling me into his private study. His appearance at the college was in itself a rare event, since he had been appointed private chaplain to my aunt Queen Anne.

The day was wet and dreary. The oak-panelled study appeared dark and forbidding, as I hesitated on the threshold. The dean told me to come on in, and to close the door behind me. He seemed older and more aggrieved than I had ever seen him before. He sat down at his desk and fixed his gaze firmly on its waxed surface.

All I could think was that I must have done something wrong, something to displease him. That I was about to be punished. But no such luck.

Instead, he began ruefully:

"I have the painful duty to inform you that your Aunt Anne, Queen of England, and her brother George, Viscount Rochford, your father, stand accused of abominable crimes, the nature of which I shall spare you."

My instant response was that some terrible misconception was afoot.

"That can't be right, sir," I argued, forgetting all about the dean's normally undisputed authority. "They are both deeply religious. Honourable and righteous. They share my conviction that we are all personally answerable to God."

Mr Parker gave me a look brimming with pity and said, in a tremulous voice:

"They have both been condemned to death."

Some part of me still refused to believe him.

"For what crime?" I asked boldly.

"High treason," the dean mumbled. "Plotting against the king."

"That's impossible!" I heard myself protest wildly. "They are both devoted to the king! They would never do anything to harm him!"

Mr Parker looked at me deploringly, his face grey in the dim light.

"This can only be a plot," I concluded, "laid by their enemies at court!"

Sounding no less distraught than I felt myself, the dean added that the charges preferred against my aunt and father had been based on information elicited by Mr Cromwell from none other than ..."

Here his voice failed him. He had to clear his voice once, then twice, before he was able to reveal that the information had been furnished by none other than his own kinswoman: Viscountess Rochford. Jane Boleyn.

My mother?

"No!" I cried in a shrill voice, back to being a helpless child. "No!"

Mr Parker did his best to be sympathetic. "Boleyn," he sighed. "I'm giving you the rest of the day off."

* * *

That was how my childhood ended. I was eleven years old. Up until then I had led a sheltered life, safe in the belief that the world was a good place to be, a place ruled by fairness and justice, where bad things did not happen to good people. The shattering of that illusion was nearly as devastating as the gruesome thought of my aunt and father being sent to the scaffold.

To avoid having to face any of my fellow students, I slipped out of the back gate to the college and made off along a muddy farm track. Not caring where it led, I marched on briskly, as if the compulsive movement would somehow distance me from the turmoil of feelings inside me. I would have preferred to run but feared it would attract attention.

Seeing a couple of farmhands on their way in my direction, I veered off across the fields. I kept going until my feet blistered and my legs felt they could carry me no longer. My breath was short and rasping. Having reached a secluded bend in the river Stour, I sank down on the bank. It was raining, and I welcomed the drops hitting my cheeks as a license for my tears to flow freely.

Bereft and bewildered, I brooded over the sudden downfall of my kin. I was in no doubt that it was not of their own making but engineered by some evil force out to destroy them, perhaps destroy us all. I asked myself how such a thing could have happened. How could God allow it? Was he not a loving God, there to protect those who believed in Him?

All I had been taught in the past year about faith and conscience, love and charity, struck me as a cruel mockery. If God existed as the benevolent Father in Heaven that he made himself out to be, how could he have abandoned good Christians like my aunt and father? How could he have got my mother involved in this ill deed? Did he not give a damn about righteousness? Worse still – was he there at all?

This latest thought was so shocking, it sent shivers down my spine. If I doubted God's existence – or even his good will – there was no way I could continue my studies to be a priest. It would eliminate my prospect for the future – the only one I had.

And there was nothing I could do about it. In the face of my present reality, I could feel my faith slipping away, leaving me with nothing but a gaping vacuity.

I don't know how long I remained sitting there, gazing unseeing out over the flat, wide-open landscape. I remember slowly becoming aware of the pungent aroma of a blooming bird cherry nearby, and somewhere behind it, the reassuring whoosh of the swollen river. A family of ducks swam past, their contented clucking mingling with birdsong.

I noticed the rain had stopped. Then all of a sudden a rift opened in the thick cloud cover, admitting a streak of gleaming afternoon sunshine. It painted the corn fields bright yellow, coloured the river azure blue. On the opposite bank, it glistened on the tender greenery of some young birches still wet from the rain.

As I sat there, lulled by the numbness inside me, the spirit of my surroundings seemed to come alive before me, like a shimmering apparition, trembling timorously in the moist air. And then something wondrous happened. It was as if a cloak of soft warm velvet had been wrapped around me. I felt suffused by goodness, imbued by great strength. What could have brought on this feeling of immense comfort? I asked myself. Could it be... mercy? Could it be... grace? Concepts I had heard discussed in class but never fully grasped. Not until now.

* * *

Throughout life I looked back on this experience on the bank of the river Stour in Suffolk as my Damascus. It formed the basis of my personal religion and carried me through many turns of profound contemplation. I came to the conclusion that God's love does not manifest itself by ensuring that our passage through life is invariably smooth and trouble-free, void of pain and suffering. Instead, His supreme gift to mankind – like that of any good parent – was that of infinite freedom. Freedom to determine for ourselves how we want to conduct our lives, within the parameters given.

It also helped me define my understanding of good and evil. Free will contained the potential of both: like two faces of the same coin, one couldn't exist without the other. We might even have to suffer evil in order to love what's good.

It made me wonder what kind of wickedness my father might have encountered, to make him wish for me to "bring some good into the world"?

My first confrontation with evil had alerted me to the goodness residing within myself. That was enough to convince me that, however bad the world around me turned out to be, I need not be tainted by it. The pain of losing my loved ones so cruelly would always be with me, but it would be tempered by the goodness I myself was able to generate.

Luckily, in the years that followed, I had no difficulty reconciling my own experience of religion with the doctrine of the reformed church. If anything, it strengthened my vocation.

I call it luck, for I could not have compromised my own stance to fit in with another system.

At college, reading the Bible as well as newly published works by Luther, Erasmus and Tyndale, I set out to raise questions, sometimes to the exasperation of my tutors. But the conclusion I reached each time was that, on principle, I was in agreement.

It was all thanks to His Majesty King Henry VIII that the reformation of the church came about, even though I shared the scepticism of many regarding his motives, counting avarice and self-will as stronger draws than religious conviction. Be that as it may, I never doubted that the New Religion gave England a chance to develop into a better country for everyone concerned.

Although at heart I disapproved of the king's drastic measures to dissolve the monasteries, rob them of images and idols that were regarded as sacred and ban rituals that formed an essential part of the nation's spiritual life, I fully agreed that we could do without the control of an autocratic pope, without priests fostering fear rather than neighbourly love, without humiliating penances and expensive indulgencies. As for the much-debated miracle of transubstantiation, I held the view that the communicants' inner experience of the Eucharist was what mattered, not what might or might not be contained in wafer and wine.

I never wished to be part of any hierarchy. My aim was to love my neighbour, serve the sick and suffering, the grief-stricken and broken-hearted, the damaged and ill-treated; help them find within themselves the solace that can only be found in your own heart.

There are those who devote themselves to charity for the sake of their own gratification, but I hope that was not the case with me. I would have liked to do so much more than my limited resources permitted. I suffered with all those whose misery I was unable to allay. And there were many whom I could not help at all: Thomas Cranmer. My father. And Anne in her hour of need...

The Tower of London

May 1536.

The Tower again, the queen's apartments, but stripped of all accoutrements. There is a musty smell, the ceiling has a damp patch, and on one wall the plaster is peeling, falling in a heap on the floor. Although there is light outside the leaded windows, the day is heavily overcast, leaving the room dusky, lit merely by a single tallow candle on a small rough-hewn oak table.

But the throne remains, and on it Anne is seated, in modest court attire, immersed in a prayer-book. Her fine clothes are crumpled, as if they have been worn for days, even slept in. But she still wears jewellery and her usual French hood, the headdress she once introduced at court and made into highest fashion.

She is utterly and totally alone.

Then, suddenly, the door opens. The person who enters is my grandmother. Not the proud, imperious Countess of Ormond and Wiltshire normally seen by the world, but a woman aged, drawn and haggard, diminished by deep sorrow. Her attire is a non-descript grey, that of a person trying hard to go unnoticed. She walks in tentatively, as if fearing to be dismissed, and stops just inside the carefully closed door, sending a guarded look towards her daughter.

Her entrance does nothing to attract Anne's attention. She does not even look up from her book.

Keeping her distance, Elizabeth tells her, in a faltering voice, that Mr Kingston has finally relented and let her in, supposedly, she adds, because of the delay.

"Oh Anne," she gasps, "I'm so relieved! This can only mean one thing."

Her daughter glances briefly up from her book, still very distant.

"That the king is weakening in his resolve," her mother elaborates. "He'll end up giving you his royal pardon."

Anne gives a chilling, uncalled-for smile.

"Nothing of the kind."

Elizabeth ventures a bit further into the room, hovers there.

183

"The master headsman was held up by bad weather in Calais," Anne continues in the same toneless voice. "That's the only privilege I've been granted. To have my head cut by a sword, not hacked off with an axe."

She's not addressing her mother, just delivering her statement into the room.

"How can you be so complacent?" whispers Elizabeth.

Her daughter gives an almost unnoticeable shrug.

Her mother draws closer.

"My dear girl..." she says beseechingly. "I've come to beg your forgiveness."

"What for?"

"For not supporting you in your distress. It was your father who forbade me to go anywhere near you. He said, you and George had brought disgrace on the family and so we must be seen to distance ourselves from you both."

This brings no response.

"But I no longer care what he says. My place is with you. For three days I've been here, begging to be admitted."

"You needn't have bothered," says Anne equably. "I've taken my leave of you all. You and father, Mary and Jane. And George, who is dead anyway."

She heaves a deep sigh.

"They made me watch as he and the others were beheaded."

Elizabeth turns away, wincing, and it is a while before she speaks again:

"Is there anything I can do for you?" she asks gently.

"I am beyond help."

"But your daughter – dear little Elizabeth," she says eagerly. "I'll do my best to be a mother to her."

"No!" Anne cries, suddenly agitated. "You're to stay away from Elizabeth!"

"Have you no feelings left? Even for your child?"

Anne draws a deep breath, and when she speaks again, it is evident that she has found her way back to what must be a hard-won state of composure.

"Much as it pains me to know that her soft little body will never again know the warmth of her mother's embrace, I take comfort from the fact that she will always have the blessing of my love. No one can take that away from her."

"My grief knows no such comfort."

Elizabeth's voice is on the point of breaking.

"That of a mother seeing a child – two of her dear children – put to death before her eyes. Having nursed them, tended them, cared for them... Seen them grow up into proud human beings, bringing hope for the future, assurance that my blood would continue once my own days were over..."

She is unable to continue.

Without warning, the door opens and Mr Kingston, Constable of the Tower of London, appears. It seems he considers enough time has been given to this meeting, but the Countess of Wiltshire and Ormond looks at him imploringly, tears falling from her eyes. He shrugs and withdraws, closing the door behind him, and Elizabeth again turns to her daughter.

"You shouldn't be alone at a time like this," she says. "Where are the others? I'm told you're allowed to have your own women back...?"

"They are no help to me. They need consoling more than I do. I won't need them until tomorrow, when I mount the block."

Her mother can't hold back a sob. She pulls a square of muslin from her sleeve and dabs her eyes with it.

When Anne speaks again, it is in a clear, calm voice:

"Last night I felt very bitter. To be killed as punishment for horrendous crimes I didn't commit..."

"I never doubted," Elizabeth hastens to put in, "that you and George were innocent."

Her comment is ignored, suggesting this goes without saying.

"But then this morning, after I was informed of the delay, giving me one more day to live... I watched the sun rise, and with it came a new kind of light. I could see that my fate is inevitable. The end of a process I myself set in train."

"You're the victim of an evil tyrant!"

Anne looks at her mother, her black eyes lambent with a glow I have never before witnessed.

"I'm not blameless," she says.

Elizabeth dismisses it outright.

"The king," she declares, "is sacrificing you because he wants to marry another woman!"

"I made some fatal errors."

"Fatal..." Elizabeth repeats darkly.

"Like fostering the notion that Henry and I were equals."

Her mother shakes her head deprecatingly.

"How could you, born a commoner, think yourself equal to a king?"

"We could never be equal so long as I was strong and he wasn't."

Her mother has to give some thought to this.

"I remember," she says after a while, "seeing Henry as a young man. Terrified of being found wanting. Scared to death of not measuring up."

"That feeling," Anne agrees, "never left him."

Her mother allows herself the shadow of a smile.

"You, by contrast, came out of the womb bursting with confidence. Confident enough to go off abroad at the age of ten, winning the favour of two foreign queens..."

"I loved them both dearly."

"Confident enough to reject King Francis and his lecherous courtiers; refuse marriage to James Butler... give your heart to

Lord Percy… Confident enough to keep His Majesty the King of England dangling on a hook for years on end…"

"I wouldn't call it confidence," Anne states soberly. "It's faith. Faith in myself. In my life being what it is. It goes hand in hand with my faith in God."

"Perhaps faith is what Henry is lacking," ponders Elizabeth.

"Indeed. Every hour of each day he needs reassurance and confirmation that he has what it takes to be king."

"And he saw to you to provide it".

"I let him believe my strength was his. Coupled with his power it formed an instrument of formidable force. I didn't realise the danger it posed in the hands of a man so unsure of his own worth."

"A deadly force…" Elizabeth shudders. "That is now being used against you."

"I should have used my strength to rein him in. Saved those first Carthusian monks. Stopped him executing Thomas More… Bishop Fisher…"

"How do you stop a man whose need to assert himself takes precedence over human life?"

"I should have done more," Anne reiterates. "As it is I, too, have blood on my hands. I helped create a monster."

At that, the candle flickers and dies. A long silence follows, until suddenly

Elizabeth is fired by new hope:

"But Anne, you know him better than anyone. You must know how best to appeal to him. Get him to commute your sentence."

Again, her daughter gives that chilling smile that reflects neither joy nor pleasure.

"I know him far too well. There's no way he can let me live."

"You can grant him a divorce and go to a nunnery. All he wants is the freedom to marry Jane Seymour. A meek, deferential woman, who, unlike you, constitutes no challenge."

"What he wants is to restore his manhood after the setback it suffered with me."

"That's no excuse for murdering you!"

But Anne is quite clear in her mind:

"Henry and I were united in our struggle to get me to the throne. We were more obsessed with the obstacles placed in our path than we were with each other. But once our mission was accomplished, the scales fell from my eyes. I saw my husband for the man he was: weak, vain, insecure. Pitiful in his hunger to appear manly."

Elizabeth snorts.

"All that jousting that half killed him!"

"His craving for a son was not just to safeguard the dynasty. It was more a wish to show the world that he was as good a man as any other."

"Oh yes," agrees her mother with obvious disdain. "In particular the virile Francis."

"I let Henry know I despised him for his clumsy pursuit of young ladies at court. I even mocked him for it. That was very unwise, knowing as I did that, in order to function as a man, Henry above all needs to feel superior."

Elizabeth nods gravely.

"That, I believe, is not unusual."

"My contempt rendered him incapable of fulfilling his conjugal duty."

"Of begetting the son he so desperately needed?"

"For him, potency was always a problem. And his efforts of late have been lamentable. I had to resort to some of Mary's French tricks to get myself pregnant. Even then the outcome proved unviable."

"As it did with Catherine."

"Henry had to put the blame on me," Anne concludes. "And now he can't risk keeping me alive to reveal his failures to the world."

Elizabeth takes a moment to contemplate this, before turning back to her daughter:

"The country is awash with theories: plotting by the Seymours, provincial rebellion, a looming French invasion, or an alliance with the emperor secretly engineered by Cromwell... But you're telling me it all comes down to one man's anxiety about his prowess in bed?"

"Why else," says Anne blankly, "would I have to die?"

Her mother suddenly totters.

Anne remains calm. She gets up from her throne and offers it to Elizabeth, who hesitates at first, then follows her daughter's command. Anne herself settles on the floor, leaning against her mother's seated figure, as perhaps she was wont to do as a child. Elizabeth puts her arm gently around her.

After a while Anne looks up and out into the room. One thing still bothering her, she tells her mother, is the thought of those four men, as well as George, who were executed, ostensibly for her sake. Four good men going to their death knowing as well as she does that they were innocent of any criminal association with her. Why those four? Close friends and trusted associates of the king? How were they selected, by whom, and why?

"Mark Smeaton," recalls Elizabeth, "was the only one to confess. But they say he was put on the rack."

"Poor little Mark – he was not known for his courage. Why on earth would I have taken him to my bed – a lute-player with a preference for boys? And the greatest mystery of all – what could have induced Jane to make up that hideous story about George and myself?"

"I've been wracking my brains over it," her mother concurs. "My own daughter-in-law… Conspiring to have my two innocent children put to death…"

Once more, her voice fails her.

Anne shows no sign of sorrow. She is again lit by that eerie inner glow, emanating from deep inside her.

"In the small hours of this morning," she says slowly, "as I prepared myself to die… I was suddenly aware that I no longer felt any pain. No worries, no regrets. Nothing left to hope for, nothing to aspire towards. And I found peace in that."

"My darling daughter…" Elizabeth's voice breaks.

"Don't grieve for me, mother. There must be some purpose in this. Little Elizabeth may have a better chance with me out of the way. She'll be closer to her father – who knows, she may even end up on the throne of England."

She rests her head on her mother's lap.

"I don't mind dying," she says. "I have faith in my destiny."

Her mother tenderly strokes her hair.

Anne smiles serenely. "This is how I want you to remember me. Your daughter, the Queen of England."

Seeing this has been a huge comfort to me. It goes a long way to heal the wound inflicted on my heart the moment I received the horrific news that my beloved Aunt Nan and her brother, the father I barely knew, had been condemned to death.

It brings to mind the words of St. Mark: "For what shall it profit a man to gain the whole world and suffer the loss of his soul?" I understand now that Anne, though she lost the world, as in the crown of England, instead gained, or rather regained, her soul. What better fate could anyone wish for a loved one?

Some of the subsequent developments strengthened my belief that King Henry's atrocities would not go unpunished. His health deteriorated steadily after Anne's death, and his marriage to Jane Seymour, following only ten days after her execution, ended in tragedy with his new queen dying in childbirth after little more than a year of marriage. In addition, the political situation in Europe grew ever more critical, and at home one rebellion followed another.

Looking back with the benefit of my full life experience, I don't believe these calamities were due to God's finger, but an inevitable outcome of the ruthless cruelty exercised by the king. With the damage he was doing to others, he also did serious damage to himself. Just as goodness generates good fortune, wickedness attracts disaster. Sacrificing Anne killed the last of King Henry's ideal of himself as a virtuous, chivalrous knight. That act destroyed the remains of all that had once been good in him.

In the years that followed the deaths of Anne and my father, I avoided all contact with my family. It was easy enough to ignore what had happened, for no one ever spoke about it.

Anne Boleyn was never mentioned; she was committed to oblivion as if she had never been. She stood for a shameful interlude in the country's recent history that everyone wished to forget.

Ensconced at Stoke-by-Clare, devoted to my religious studies, I was mercifully cut off from life in London and the royal court. Only on one occasion, accompanying Mr Parker and my fellow-students to a service at St. Peter ad Vincula at the Tower of London, was I painfully conscious of the fact that this was where Anne and my father lay buried. The knowledge so disturbed my composure, I determined never to visit the church again.

In April 1539, I was reached by the news that my grandmother had passed away. Her health, I was told by Mr Parker, had suffered ever since Anne and my father were beheaded.

Her heart was broken, her will to live diminished, and now Death had come to deliver her.

I had to steel myself against the thought of seeing my Boleyn relations again. At least it didn't entail a return to Hever. My grandmother had elected to be buried, not with the Boleyns in St. Peter's Church, but in the Howard family chapel in St. Mary's Church in Lambeth – a sign as sure as any of her disillusionment with the family she had married into.

Mr Parker accompanied me there, and in his company I was able to remain distant and formal. The whole Howard clan was in attendance, but surprisingly few other representatives of the royal household. The disgrace tainting the Boleyns had obviously not been forgotten.

Mary was present with her husband William Stafford, and so were my cousins Henry Carey and Kitty, but I contented myself greeting them cursorily after the ceremony and then excusing myself, saying I had to travel back to Stoke-by-Clare with Mr Parker.

The event left me with mixed feelings. While I shied away from the strong feelings it evoked, I regretted not having made more of this reunion with the only kin I had left – not counting my mother, who, incidentally, had been conspicuous by her absence – I believe, to the relief of us all.

An opportunity to make amends presented itself a mere eleven months later, when it was my grandfather's turn to leave this life. This time the funeral was to be held at Hever: a place I had no wish to revisit. But Mr Parker made the decision for me, granting me a whole week of compassionate leave, and I could think of no acceptable excuse to stay away.

I arrived early, before preparations for the funeral had even started. Although my grandfather had spent most of his life away from the castle, it gave a sad, empty impression, like a place abandoned. The servants drifted about aimlessly, like boats without a rudder.

Seeing no signs of any family members, I escaped out of doors, where an early spring was presenting the grounds in their most delightful guise. The sun beamed from a clear blue sky, a rich scent emanated from the herb garden, the swards were dotted with daffodils. I crossed the drawbridge, passed the flat stone where Urian had stationed himself in faithful anticipation of his beloved mistress' return, pining away until the day he died of old age.

Down by the river, the glittering water brought to mind hot summer days: Mary in her chemise extended on a blanket, her peals of laughter as we clambered over her. Across on the other side, a track up the hill towards the oak wood reminded me of wild gallops with Anne on Augustus, and beyond the orchard I glimpsed the rough meadow where we had flown Davy her merlin. Faced with it all, I struggled with a lump in my throat.

Then suddenly I heard my name called: "Jojo" – a childish nickname I hadn't heard for years. Swivelling round, I discovered my cousin Kitty running towards me. We fell into each other's arms. No words were needed to tell that we shared the same profound sense of loss. Unable to hold back my tears, I felt them mingling on my cheeks with hers.

193

Kitty, now fifteen years old, had grown into a beautiful young lady. The mischief that had marked her as a young child had been replaced by a soulful, not to say grave, demeanour and in her eyes, a sense of loneliness akin to my own.

We crossed the river on the narrow stone bridge and went for a long walk through the oak wood. There, for the first time, I learnt the details of our dear aunt's demise. Kitty, though only twelve years old at the time, had been one of the ladies accompanying Anne to her bitter end. And as we wandered among trees sheer with tender new growth and vibrant with exuberant birdsong, she described to me Anne's courage and dignity as she calmly mounted the scaffold.

Before being blindfolded, she had turned, with a smile, to her executioner, the master headsman brought over from Calais, to hand him the customary half-crown as a token of her forgiveness. And the speech she was allowed to give before placing her head on the block was without rancour, even complimentary to His Majesty, describing him as "gentle and merciful, a good sovereign lord".

"How could she say that?" I burst out. "At that moment she could afford to be truthful."

Kitty retorted that no doubt she was speaking with little Elizabeth's best interests at heart.

"After that she prayed. She kept praying up until the end. Even after her head was severed from her body, could we see her lips moving in prayer."

I felt relieved not to have been anywhere near the Tower on this fateful day. At the same time I envied Kitty for having been present to perform that last loving act. I told her I was pleased that someone so close to Anne, someone as devoted to her as I was myself, had been with her up until her horrific end.

After Mary was banished from court, Kitty told me, Anne had become like a mother to her. And she herself felt more like Anne's daughter than just another maid of honour. It was odd, I reflected, how the Boleyn women had made a habit of mothering each other's children, as if family members were interchangeable.

I asked her about her own life since, and she told me that, for almost three years now, she had languished at Hever with only her grandmother and Grandma Butler for company. She'd had no option but to leave court, since there was no way the new queen, Jane Seymour, would have accepted a niece of Anne Boleyn as a member of her household.

"And yet your mother was favoured by her," Kitty grumbled. "She was reinstated in no time."

That was different, I reminded her. My mother had helped put Jane Seymour on the throne, by plotting against Anne and my father.

Kitty gave a shudder.

"God grant that I shall never have to serve alongside that viper of a woman. Much as I hanker to be back at court."

She had been told that this would only be possible when the king found a new wife.

"They say he is scouring the continent for a new candidate, but none of the European princesses will countenance marrying him. As one of them responded, she has but one head and she would like to keep it."

Asking her for news about the rest of our family, I learnt that our cousin little Princess Elizabeth was being well looked after by her father the king. She had her own household at Hatfield and good erudite tutors to educate, not only her, but also Kitty's brother, my cousin Henry Carey, who had been moved from the Cistercian Abbey at Syon.

"Apparently, he has become like an older brother to her. Elizabeth adores him."

"And what about your mother?" I asked. There was still room for Mary in my heart. Unconnected as she was with the Boleyn disaster, I occasionally allowed myself to think of her fondly.

Kitty replied glibly that Mary was grand, back in England after living for some time in Calais.

"She's all wrapped up in her new husband and babies."

Her tone suggested that this was something she was not altogether pleased about. It also explained why she had stayed on at Hever rather than join her mother's household.

"Do you ever see her?"

"Oh yes, she comes frequently to help care for Grandma Butler. I bet she hopes to be remembered in her will. Stafford doesn't have much to his name."

That is a bit unfair, I thought to myself. Mary was not greedy, and she had always got on well with her grandmother.

I was pleased to hear that she was expected to attend her father's funeral.

"And how is Grandma Butler these days?" I wondered. "She must be ancient by now."

Kitty reckoned she'd be well into her eighties.

"Her father lived to be ninety. It's the Ormond blood."

"Let's hope we both have plenty of it," I joked, nudging her.

We made our way across the inner courtyard, through the entrance hall and the estate office, and up the stairs in the tower to Grandma Butler's private enclave that had been out of bounds to us as children.

"Will we be welcome?" I asked anxiously, but Kitty reassured me that, nowadays, our great-grandmother rather liked to have visits.

"I suppose she's away with the fairies?"

My belief was that elderly people lost their mind when reality became too much for them. And in her old age, Grandma Butler had had more than her fair share to contend with.

"See for yourself," was Kitty's reply.

This was my first ever visit to Grandma Butler's bedroom, and my first impression was the darkness of it: oak-panelled walls, hangings in muted colours and coloured plates of glass in the leaded windows obscuring most of the bright spring sunshine outside.

Our great-grandmother was sitting up in the heavily carved four-poster bed, staring straight ahead. Even smaller than I remembered her, reduced to skin and bone, she was perfectly still. At first I felt sad at the thought of her spending her days and nights bed-bound and surrounded by all this gloom, but then I noticed, first her hands: painfully gnarled fingers drumming reflectively on the bedcover, and then her eyes: as shining black and alert as ever, suggesting that, however enfeebled her flesh, Grandma Butler's mind was far from idle.

Our polite condolences were gracefully accepted. Losing a child, and especially a favourite son, was a cruel blow, she said, but her grief was mitigated by the thought that she would soon be joining him.

She made it sound like something she was looking forward to.

At her suggestion, we sat down on the two chairs in the room. As we went on chatting, Grandma Butler revealed a surprising lucidity, healthily free of illusion, especially as regarded three of her grandchildren, one of whom she seemed to hold in higher esteem than the others.

"Mary was the one who got it right," she declared. "And mark my word – she was the one who survived."

She went on to say that the poor child should never have been sent off to France so young and without a proper escort. What was her son Thomas thinking, leaving a young girl exposed and unprotected amongst a horde of libidinous French courtiers?

"I told Thomas as much. He should have known better. This is how all abuse happens – its prey the lost and lonely!"

Her words made little sense to my cousin and myself, ignorant as we were of Mary's French exploits.

"My mother is very happy now," Kitty ventured, though again I detected that hint of disapproval in her voice.

"And well she should be! Mary is worth every ounce of happiness she can get. Because you see, she let herself be guided by her values, and that, my children, is the key to success in life!"

Kitty and I waited in silence, while our great-grandmother briefly fell back into thought, her fingers drumming vigorously.

"The boy now, young George..." she went on after a while. "So well endowed – clever, good-looking, well-mannered. It begs the question – where did he go wrong?"

She looked at us searchingly, inviting an answer.

"Perhaps he didn't go wrong at all," Kitty proposed. "I think he was a victim of circumstance."

"No such thing," Grandma Butler scoffed. "I have lived long enough to know that everything that happens is a result of our own actions."

"Even when others take measures to serve their own interests?" I put in bravely, having learnt at Stoke-by-Clare to hold my own in discussions.

It met with no response.

"George was basically a good lad, but he was..." our great-grandmother searched for a word. "Impetuous. That's it. As a small child, I often noticed him being rash, even reckless. I chided him for it. 'You cannot allow yourself to give in to impulse!' I kept telling him. 'Sooner or later it will land you in trouble.'"

I tried in vain to work out how impulse could have landed my father on the block.

"Not that he paid a blind bit of attention," Grandma Butler concluded.

As if listening to his grandmother would have saved him.

"Now Anne..." she held forth. "When she started to get above herself, I tried to talk some sense into her. 'No trees grow to heaven,' I warned her. For all the good it did, I might as well have saved my breath."

A brief toss of her head revealed her displeasure:

"There was a time when I advised her to surrender control of her life. As I saw it, the powers at play weighed in more heavily than personal interest. In due course, she took my advice. What I hadn't expected was that, in the process, she lost the run of herself."

She peered at us with those uncanny black eyes, so like Anne's, that seemed to look right through you.

"That's why it all went wrong. Remember that," she told us. "Whatever happens to you, hold on to your own self. For without it, you founder."

"That's a lot of wisdom to be getting on with," I said, getting up from my chair, seized by a sudden desire to escape back out into the sunshine.

Grandma Butler nodded sagaciously.

"It's the perspective afforded by old age. To compensate you for the failing of other faculties. I'm glad the good Lord let me live for long enough to see things for what they are worth. Regretting only that it took me so long."

I didn't have the heart to point out that there was still much in our joint history that was beyond comprehension for us all.

Feeling this was a good time to leave, I made for the tower, but just as I reached it, my great-grandmother's next utterance stopped me in my tracks.

"As regards Jane... your mother..." she began. "Pure poison. If only George hadn't married her!"

Torn between escaping and coming back into the room, I lingered where I was.

"I'm glad to say," she went on, "that she has written to say she does not wish to attend the funeral of her father-in-law. In any case, she wouldn't have been welcome! After all the devastation she's brought to this family... I would have shown her the door, had she had the gall to show up here."

Intrigued by this spurt of antagonism, I sat down again.

"My son's last few months were made hell by her. I'm in no doubt that she foreshortened his life."

Kitty, too, was paying attention now. "Why? What did Jane do?"

Apparently she had caused great concern obstructing a deal over some Ormond properties belonging to Grandma Butler, the income of which had been pledged to my mother in a jointure on her marriage to protect her in case of widowhood. An extremely lucrative offer had been extended for these Buckinghamshire manors, but for conveyance to go through, Jane had to formally relinquish her interest in these properties. In return, our grandfather had made her a generous offer of an alternative asset that would bring her an increased annual income. Realizing that the deal depended on her agreement, Jane had taken full advantage, insisting on greater rewards.

Haggling had gone on for many months, leaving our grandfather exasperated, at risk of losing the promising deal, as the buyer was losing patience. Jane held out. She even resorted to scheming behind his back, obtaining an Act of Parliament to safeguard her interests.

"How did she manage that?" I asked, reluctantly impressed by my mother's acumen.

"By appealing to Cromwell, her protector of old. A close friend of her father's. She's been in his good books ever since she accommodated him over Anne and George."

Of course. An old debt being repaid.

"In the end we had to give her Blickling, our own former home – though only for her lifetime. With that, and the income from her new settlement, she'd extracted all she could from the Boleyns."

While my great-grandmother obviously begrudged her every penny, my feeling was that no price would have been too high to keep my mother off our backs. With luck, her improved new circumstances might save us from ever seeing or hearing of her again.

Whitehall Palace

May 1540.

Heavy traffic of barges suggests the Thames, somewhere in the middle of London. Grounds well tended, as for a royal palace, and in the background a massive edifice covered in scaffolds: all adding up to Whitehall Palace, the rebuilding of which went on for decades after an army of carpenters, stonemasons, glaziers, painters and seamstresses finished their work of removing, deleting and obliterating every trace of Queen Anne's presence there.

It looks like a splendid morning in late spring: the river glittering in bright sunshine slanting through the tall chestnut trees planted in Cardinal Wolsey's time; the air fragrant from their blossom; birds' twitter above the sound of workmen hammering and boatmen hollering on the river.

And there I see my cousin Kitty, beautifully attired in court attire, pleased to partake of the fresh morning air. Then footsteps are heard hastily approaching. She turns round, noting with some dismay the appearance of my mother Jane.

"Kitty – I need to talk to you. In private."

She indicates a bench in the middle of a sward, the kind of place you choose to be out of earshot but with a clear view of anyone coming near. Jane goes over and sits down, patting the bench next to her. Kitty joins her with obvious reluctance. She doesn't sit down but remains standing.

Jane starts off affably enough:

"Please accept my congratulations on your marriage."

Kitty gives a curt bow of acknowledgement.

"I'm told it's a love match."

"I wouldn't have considered anything less."

That's the Boleyn blood speaking! She sounds just like our Aunt Nan. Who probably had it from Grandma Butler.

"I believe your husband has the ear of the king."

That is enough to put Kitty instantly on guard.

"I want him to intervene with His Majesty. On behalf of Mr Cromwell."

Kitty's eyebrows shoot up in astonishment.

"Mr Cromwell is far closer to the king than my husband will ever be."

"Not anymore. Haven't you heard? He is about to be arrested. Most likely executed."

"Whatever for?"

"For tricking the king into marrying a woman so hideous he can't bring himself to perform his conjugal duty."

The absurdity of this strikes Kitty as amusing.

"Anna of Cleves is not hideous. And the king himself chose to marry her."

"That was on the strength of Holbein's portrait. Mr Holbein, too, is in trouble over that."

"At court blame is always apportioned," my cousin comments – cynically, for someone so young.

"Well I'm being blamed, too. By Cromwell."

Kitty's attention is drawn to the river, where one barge has collided with another and a furious row has erupted between the boatmen.

"Please, Kitty," my mother enjoins her, "do sit down."

She waits for my cousin to do so, stiffly, at the far end of the bench, before continuing:

"Cromwell allotted me the task of making the queen appeal to His Highness. I did all in my power: washed her, scented her, dressed her hair, swathed her in the most ravishing night shift of black lace... Instructed her, as well as I could, in the art of seduction. I could have done with your mother's advice there," Jane adds tartly.

Seeing that her last remark did not go down very well, she quickly resumes:

"And all to no avail! The morning after the wedding night, when I asked the new queen how she'd got on, she replied that the king has held her hand and kissed her on the cheek. Did that mean she was now pregnant?"

"She was having you on, Jane. No woman is as ignorant as that."

"The marriage remains unconsummated. And Cromwell says it is up to me to make Anna irresistible to the king. But I've done all I can. I'm at my wits' end!"

Kitty offers her personal view on the matter.

"There's nothing you or Anna can do."

It draws an immediate reaction.

"What do you know about it?"

"I was there," says Kitty. "At Rochester."

And so, with the odd prompting and query from my mother, the whole sorry saga is unfolded:

Kitty had been sent as part of the retinue to welcome Anna of Cleves on her arrival from the Continent. They had been detained for weeks in Dover, as bad weather precluded a crossing of the English Channel from Calais.

Momentarily distracted, my cousin mentions that this was how she met her husband. Francis Knollys was another member of the receiving committee, as was her stepfather William Stafford, who introduced the two of them.

Jane is not interested. She wants to hear about Anna of Cleves. So Kitty goes on to tell how the prospective queen finally arrived with a handful of German attendants, one of whom spoke good enough English to act as interpreter. The party were taken to nearby Rochester Priory for a rest before going on to London. The English hosts found Anna nice and comely, not at all unattractive, if tall and curvy and with a few pockmarks on her face. More importantly, her manner was kindly and pleasant.

A messenger had been despatched to Greenwich to inform the king that his bride had arrived safely on English shores and would be escorted to the royal residence within the next few days. However, His Majesty, unable to contain his curiosity, decided on an unconventional, light-hearted introduction. Together with a few high-spirited associates, he rode post to

Rochester and, disguised as Robin Hood with his Merry Men, burst into the chamber where Anna and her ladies were watching bull-baiting from the windows. King Henry rushed up to his intended, grabbed her by the waist and planted a wet kiss on her lips.

Terrified, Anna screamed and called out in German for guards to come to her rescue, something to the effect of forcibly expelling the impostors. Booming with laughter, His Majesty threw off his cloak and hood with an extravagant gesture, bowed deeply and imparted the news that the rogue facing her was in fact her king and about-to-be husband.

His behaviour was that of a handsome, chivalrous knight wooing the lucky lady of his choosing. But as Anna stared at him transfixed, her expression could be seen shifting from abject horror to one of utter revulsion.

The memory of it makes Kitty cringe.

"Oh, it was painful to see the king so humiliated. He literally shrank under that stare. It was a good while before he managed to pull himself up, turn away and mutter to his attendants: 'I like her not.'"

Of course. Blame was always apportioned.

Jane reflects for a moment, then concludes that His Royal Highness must have got over it, since the marriage took place only a few days later.

"Only because he was anxious to have the Duke of Cleves as an ally against the new triple alliance between Spain and France and the Vatican. Perhaps he nursed a hope that the wedding night would sort things out."

"Well we all know that didn't happen."

Standing up to check that they cannot be overheard, Kitty passes on to Jane, in a low voice, something that our Aunt Nan had confided in her mother, who in turn passed it on to her granddaughter: that the king could only perform with a woman if he felt admired.

"Anna's reaction in Rochester is something he can't ignore. The knowledge that she finds him repulsive is what's keeping him from fulfilling his marital duties."

"And he intends to punish poor Mr Cromwell for it!"

"Anything to save face."

"That's not fair!" Jane cries, getting to her feet. "Something must be done to save him!"

"Why are you so concerned about Cromwell?" asks Kitty. "The man is a beast. He deserves whatever he gets."

"He has never been anything but good to me," Jane protests. "He's been my bridge to the king's favour."

It draws a scathing reply:

"You mean he's been doing you favours in return for favours you've done for him?"

"Well that's how things work."

"Only for some."

My cousin turns her back and starts walking away, suggesting this conversation has come to an end. But Jane follows, falling into step with her.

"Don't you see, Kitty, this is in your interest as well! If Anna is sent away, we will both lose our positions at court. We'll need Mr Cromwell there to plead for us."

Having reached the embankment, Kitty has stopped to look out over the water. The irate boatmen have gone their separate ways; on the opposite bank a boat is being unloaded at a quay by a grand house further down the Strand, a party of ladies are being helped ashore.

Hovering next to her, Jane is awaiting a response.

At length it comes:

"Have you not noticed what's going on at court?"

Jane blanches. Has she missed something?

"With Katheryn Howard."

A laugh of relief from Jane:

"You mean the king's laughable efforts to convince himself and everyone else that the failure of his new marriage is due to no failure on his part?"

"Yes."

"No one could fail to notice him making a fool of himself with little Katheryn. Pretending to be an attractive young stud, not a flabby old fart, with breath bad enough to kill and a leg sore stinking to high heaven – "

"Shh!" Kitty interrupts her, looking cautiously around. "Such talk is treasonous!"

"Katheryn probably reminds him of your mother," Jane suggests, "in her bloom of youth."

"My mother was never that giddy!" Kitty objects. "But at least Katheryn has the sense to respond as if this decrepit old wreck is God's gift to women."

Jane shrugs.

"So King Henry has a new mistress. Good luck to him. It means he can stay married to Anna and Cromwell gets to keep his head."

Again with Kitty leading, they start to walk along the river, where a soft breeze stirs the candle blossom of the chestnut trees and ruffles the silk of Kitty's elaborate sleeves.

Looking out over the water, she says blithely:

"The king wants to marry her."

"Marry? Katheryn Howard? That silly wisp of a girl?"

Kitty nods knowingly.

"Who told you that?"

"My husband. Who had it from His Majesty himself."

Seeing Jane struggling with this piece of information, Kitty adds: "The marriage to Anna will have to be annulled."

"What about political support from Cleves?"

"Francis and Charles are at logger-heads again, so the threat of a joint invasion has receded."

Jane remains doubtful.

"Has the king forgotten what he went through to get rid of his first wife?"

"This time it will be easy."

A subtle shift has occurred in the balance between these two women. Kitty, though so much younger, is now the one in command.

"Listen Jane," she says, her voice firm and level. "If my darling husband were to inform the king that you are willing to testify –"

"Testify? To what?"

"That his marriage to Anna was never consummated –"

"You mean, by repeating what the queen told me?"

"It will help the king get his annulment. You will have his eternal gratitude. No more need for a bridge to his favour."

Jane is thinking hard.

"And what about Mr Cromwell?"

"He'll be left to the hands of divine justice."

As they walk back to the palace, Jane remains deep in thought. Another question occurs to her:

"If I may ask... What is your interest in seeing Katheryn Howard on the throne?"

Suspicion is written all over her. Having spent more than two decades at the English court, she knows that very little happens there without hidden motives.

Kitty smiles, the smile of someone who knows she's on the winning side.

"Have you forgotten, Jane? She's my own dear cousin."

In life, I often marvelled at the way major world events had the capacity to reach deep into the lives of innocent, unconnected individuals. During my childhood, whereas the intricate mesh of international politics affected the power of balance in Europe, it also reverberated through the walls of our small castle in Kent, tolling the bell for all of us there. And there was hardly a person in England who had not been in some way affected.

Presently, however, I find myself more fascinated by the capacity of single individuals to affect the course of world history – and rarely for the best of reasons.

There is good and bad in all of us, but in positions of power and authority, flaws in the character seem to take over. Our world might have been a better place, had it not been for the self-absorption of Emperor Charles V, the immorality of King Francis I, the duplicity of Pope Clement VII... Not to mention our own King Henry VIII, who stopped at nothing to cover up his own feelings of inadequacy. The acquisitive Cardinal Wolsey and the pitiless Thomas Cromwell inflicted further damage to our country. As for women: if Queen Catherine of Aragon had tempered her wilful Spanish pride, if Anne had not allowed herself to become so haughty and condescending... If little Catherine Howard had been less wanton, if my mother's final elevation had not gone to her head...

But this is all fruitless speculation. What it comes down to is that power corrupts. More to the point: what do ordinary people, of little or no power, have to set against such fallibility? I suppose, only their own personal convictions, the best each of them can offer, on the premise that, sooner or later, the weight of combined effort will make up for the lack of clout.

Sudden wealth can also be a challenge, as I learnt myself at the age of fourteen, when it transpired that in his will my grandfather Thomas Boleyn had named me as his heir-general. My first reaction was immense surprise: in life, he had never paid any attention to me. But, as Mary equably pointed out, I was the son of his only son surviving into adulthood – who else was there to inherit? Only yourself, I thought, but that obviously hadn't occurred to her. Mary accepted that, as a woman, she didn't enter into the equation.

Still, she had not been forgotten. Under the will she was given ownership of Rochford Manor, which would be a great improvement on William Stafford's farmhouse. Furthermore, as long as I remained a minor, she would be my guardian and manage my affairs. This pleased me, as it would bring me into closer contact with her.

Less appealing was the discovery that, as heir-general, I was now responsible for my mother's affairs! To my relief, these could be delegated to my aunt/guardian – an arrangement gleefully approved by my mother. She suspected no doubt – rightly, as it turned out – that Mary would prove a soft touch. I didn't mind, as long as I didn't have to deal with her.

It took me a while to get used to the idea of being a rich young man, but when I did, I discovered that wealth meant very little to me. Much as I appreciated the recognition and the trust my grandfather had placed in me by making me his heir, I worried that having to take charge of all his diverse properties, manors and farms, would detract from my main ambition: to serve the church: in my father's words "bring some good into the world".

It was just as well that I took this view, for my grandfather was not long in his grave, when King Henry started to make overtures to Mary claiming royal ownership of most of his estate. It was contended that the manors granted to my grandfather had been only for his lifetime, not for passing on to a next generation. In addition, according to the king, all my grandfather's foreign travel had been financed by loans out of the royal coffers, and these were now due for repayment.

Much of this could have been met with counter claims. Deeds to properties were in my grandfather's name and so legal proof of ownership. The diplomatic missions abroad had been

214

undertaken on behalf of the crown, and so on. But Mary was not going to argue with her sovereign. She agreed to his repossession of all those properties he had once given away.

What was left to me, my grandfather's personal possessions and his papers, was enough to satisfy me. I didn't need all those manors. As a man of the cloth I would always be accommodated by the church. There was also enough money to continue my education and to pay my mother her pension, as well as a small capital to keep as security, in case of the unexpected.

When Grandma Butler died shortly after her son, she left most of the vast Butler fortune to her favourite grandchild, that is, Mary. No nonsense here of prioritising male heirs. Had not she and her sister been the sole beneficiaries of the great wealth left by her father, the seventh Earl of Ormónd? Only Hever Castle she left to her son William.

It pleased me to think that Mary, who had once placed love – or values, as her grandmother put it – before material concerns, had ended up with a fortune on her hands. She was the one who had got it all. Now there, I said to myself, is a nice moral lesson.

However, the lesson ended tragically, for Mary's life was cut short by an outbreak of plague only a few years after her circumstances changed so dramatically.

Perhaps we're not meant to have it all.

* * *

This brings to mind the church warden of a small parish in Nottinghamshire, where I served as curate after leaving Cambridge. The yeoman was a dour character, enlivened only by his devout adherence to the New Religion. He and I had some interesting discussions on the subject, particularly poignant at this juncture.

I helped officiate at his wedding. He married belatedly a lovely woman decades younger than himself, in fact the daughter of a neighbour, of the same persuasion, so as to pre-empt any religious dissension in the household. To me he had confided that he felt no desire for a woman in his life but wished to have an heir to keep his property from falling into the hands of a feckless Catholic nephew.

These hopes of his were, however, dashed only a few months later by a near-fatal encounter with a run-away bull that left him paralysed from the waist down. From then on he was unable to attend church services, as was his wife Beatrice, whom he wouldn't let out of his sight. I therefore got into the habit of visiting their home to preach and give them both Holy Communion.

I greatly admired Beatrice for the care she provided for this invalid, who only grew increasingly gruff and bad-tempered, impatient with her tender ministrations. Invariably kind and gentle, she never uttered a word of complaint. But though she concealed it well, I detected beneath the surface the deep dolour of hopelessness and disillusion.

When, after three years, her husband passed away, I sensed her grief, not so much mourning his passing as mourning all that her marriage had failed to deliver. What can be more tragic than losing what you never had? I could not help being moved – feeling her sorrow as keenly as if it had been my own.

With scant experience in matters of the heart, I never surmised that such intuitive sympathy is a true manifestation of love. For the same reason, it never occurred to me that my feelings could possibly be reciprocated. I had long since accepted that I would spend my life married only to my vocation. Not because of mandatory celibacy for priests – that was all changed with the New Religion. Archbishop Thomas Cranmer himself has married not once, but twice! It was more to compensate for the fact that, in my view, no woman in her right mind would choose to become a member of my infamous family. To save myself the pain of rejection, I closed my mind to the prospect that some woman might find within her enough affection for my person to outweigh the dictates of good sense.

Meanwhile, dramatic changes were taking place in England: turmoil that had been initiated by the death of King Henry VIII. His immediate heir, his only son by Jane Seymour, the boy king Edward VI, turned out to be a religious fanatic – but at least he was a fellow Protestant. Still – young Edward was an innocent compared to his rabid Catholic half-sister and godmother. Following the young king's premature death, Mary Tudor swiftly eliminated his appointed successor, Lady Jane Grey, and seized the crown for herself.

It has to be admitted that King Henry's eldest daughter, had not had an easy life. Princess Mary had seen her dear mother, Catherine of Aragon, derogated, banished from court and left to an early death in a comfortless remote castle. From having started her life as a pampered royal princess with a splendid future ahead, Mary Tudor had been declared a bastard and stripped of her royal status. The French had made things worse by reneging on the proposed marriage between her and the *dauphin*.

The one thing to sustain Catherine of Aragon had been her staunch Catholic faith, and Mary, brought up to the same ethos, did her best to emulate her mother's degree of piety. However, once she reached the throne, devotion was replaced by vengeance: an obsessive hatred directed against Protestants, clergy-men and – perhaps most of all – the Boleyn family.

At the end of her life, Anne said that one thing she regretted was the cruel treatment her stepdaughter had suffered while she was queen. Though Henry was the instigator, it was no doubt encouraged by herself. After Anne's death, Mary had elected to put the entire blame at her stepmother's door as a means to resurrect the ailing relationship with her father.

In the spring of 1554, I was greatly concerned by the news that Anne's daughter, Princess Elizabeth, had been imprisoned in the Tower. I had only met this cousin of mine on one occasion, when she came with her father the king to attend our grandfather's funeral at Hever. Though only five years old at the time, she had witnessed his interment with all the dignity and solemnity you would have expected from a much older child. It had endeared her to me, and ever since I had followed her life from afar. Now, with her half-sister Mary on the throne, I could only pray that the queen's vitriol would not spill over on Anne's blameless young daughter.

At this time, many well-heeled Protestants reckoned there was only one safe option open to them: to leave England. Among my own relations, Kitty and her family had gone to live in Germany; William Stafford with his children by Mary was in Switzerland. Henry Carey, still in England, was hopefully safe as a successful politician: Member of Parliament for Buckingham.

I was truly horrified to hear reports that irreproachable churchmen were being burnt at the stake in London. Even the archbishop Thomas Cranmer did not escape. In order to save his life, he had gone as far as to make several recantations, but Queen Mary still pressed ahead with his execution. Before the fire was lit, he withdrew his recantation, preferring to die a heretic.

"You shouldn't stay here," Beatrice told me on one occasion after a service in the church, where she had taken over some of the duties once performed by her husband. "England isn't safe for you."

She was right. A Protestant clergyman and a Boleyn to boot, I was in immediate danger. Yet something held me back. And as the reason for this suddenly dawned upon me, I saw no reason to keep it to myself.

"I wouldn't want to leave you."

Beatrice looked up. And deep in her eye I noticed a light, a shy flame of hope, of warmth, of kindness – or could it, might it, possibly be love?

What she said was:

"You can always you take me with you."

And so, on a gloomy day in November, 1555, we became man and wife, in our own little church, where we had spent endless hours happy in each other's company, doing mundane tasks like dusting pews, sweeping out aisles, polishing memorials and replacing burnt-down candles, never thinking for a moment that one day we would have more essential things to share.

There was nothing to keep us in England. I had no property left – the only place where I would have liked to live was Hever Castle, but it had been claimed by the crown and given to Anna of Cleves as part of her divorce settlement. As for Beatrice's manor, this had been claimed by the feckless nephew, and she had had to go back and live with her miserly old father. So we both had good reason to look further afield.

From Protestants escaping to the Continent came reports that they had serious problems with things like shortage of accommodation, financial exploitation and language barriers. So instead, Beatrice and I crossed over to Ireland. Steering clear of the east coast, where the Pale formed the base of English rule, we headed for the peaceful counties further inland. Right in the heart of the island, we found a tower house for sale: Clonony Castle, a sturdy edifice, three stories high, built only some fifty years earlier, in a lovely open position with just enough land to sustain us and the healthy river Brosna running through it. The remainder of my inheritance secured it for us.

Clonony did not have the home comforts Beatrice had been used to, and it compared poorly with Hever, but we soon learnt to manage with whatever was at hand. The one thing I regretted was not being able to preach the new gospel beyond the walls of the castle – it wasn't considered safe, and I was not prepared to expose my wife to any danger. Still – Clonony was where the best days of my life were spent. Beatrice and I lived quietly, largely self-sufficient, spending our days tending crops and livestock. Within a year our son Thomas was born, and as we devoted ourselves to caring for him and each other, I felt my cup was running over. At the end of each day came the bliss of going to sleep in the arms of a beloved: an exquisite pleasure I had not known since I was a toddler and my Aunt Mary took me to her bed at night.

At Clonony, like Mary, I had it all.

And like Mary, I soon lost it.

My darling Beatrice passed away giving birth to our second child: a little girl, who perished with her.

I thought at first that my heart would break, that I would never find my feet again. But then I remembered Beatrice's bitter grief when she herself was bereaved. Unlike her, I had been left with the glorious memory of having loved, and of being loved in return. I found comfort in the fact that, on balance, I had gained more than I had lost.

Not to forget, she had given me Thomas. From the day he was born, I had endeavoured to be to him the father I had never known myself. Now I had to go a step further and be both mother and father to him. In return I had his devotion and, in due course, three delightful granddaughters: according to my wishes, named Anne, Mary and Elizabeth, after my dearly beloved aunts and grandmother.

My affection for them all gave meaning to my life. And yet... they seem distant now. I can barely recall their faces. Nothing holds them to me: no doubt, no regrets, no wisp of a shadow. Love, when fulfilled, knows only gratitude.

* * *

After Queen Mary mercifully died and Elizabeth ascended the throne, making her country Protestant once more, we were able to return to England. But I kept Clonony, where Beatrice's spirit remained very much in evidence. Thomas always regarded the castle as his home, and in due course this was where he chose to settle, to bring up his family.

Of my Boleyn cousins, Elizabeth is the only one to have survived me. At the age of twenty-five, she was the only candidate left for the throne of England. And what a formidable monarch she proved to be. Under her reign, our country has flourished as never before.

She showed a particular fondness for Mary's two eldest children, presumably due to the link they formed to the unfortunate mother she hardly knew. Kitty became her close confidante and was appointed Chief Lady of the Bed Chamber, the highest office for a woman at court.

Having married for love, Kitty enjoyed a happy marriage. She gave birth to fourteen children, but all those pregnancies took their toll on her health and she passed away aged only forty-five, leaving all her kin inconsolable, I think most of all Queen Elizabeth herself.

I'd be interested to know who was Kitty's father: Mary's husband William Carey or His Majesty King Henry? Mary herself never let on.

Conversely, the paternity of her brother Henry Carey was never in doubt. He looked so much like his father the king, though I'm glad to say, his character owed more to his sweet mother. After being reunited at our grandfather's funeral, we became firm friends for life. He showed his trust appointing me executor of his will.

Elizabeth treated him like the brother that indeed he was. Early on in her reign she ennobled him as Baron Hunsdon and gave him Hunsdon Manor in homage to happy childhood times they had spent there together. As a court favourite, he was honoured with eminent royal appointments, ending up as her Lord Chamberlain.

Cousin Henry lived to a ripe old age, having sired no less than sixteen children, as well as a few on the other side of the blanket. So the line laid by Mary and King Henry VIII looks set to continue.

I'm struck by the fact that neither of my two departed cousins has shown up here in the sphere of light. Perhaps they were lucky enough to have everything resolved, and so able to progress unimpeded.

That's more than I can say for myself. I am still battling with a major conundrum: that of my mother Jane. What on earth was she up to with our other cousin, little Katheryn Howard, who became Queen of England after King Henry divorced Anna of Cleves? The poor girl could have done without my mother's ministrations. Like my Aunt Mary, she had been used as a plaything by lecherous grown men, made to believe that was all she was good for.

At least my aunt finally had the good fortune to end up with a man worthy of her love. Little Katheryn had no such luck.

But what was my mother's role in a game that could only lead to her own brutal downfall?

They say she was out of her mind. Mad as a march hare.

Was she mad?

I 'm not convinced...

A London Square

January 1542.

A square, by the looks of it somewhere in London: squalid, low-built houses, mucky pavements and gutters. It's a cold, raw winter's day, freezing fog lingering like smoke in the narrow alleys leading off the square. Horses, mules, the odd donkey, all contribute to the general filth: heaps of fresh manure steam in the cold air.

In spite of the cold, there are plenty of people about: fishwives and farmers selling their produce, a few men and women queuing up to draw water from the well, others in a huddle exchanging gossip. I see them shivering, stamping their feet, rubbing their hands together. Then suddenly their attention is drawn to a new arrival, and all efforts to keep warm are forgotten.

The fellow is small and wiry. A sly look on his face coupled with a mat of red fur on his head brings to mind a fox. Slung across his back is a lute. My heart sinks. There is no item I more detest seeing, prone as they are to accompany some abominable rhymes relating to my nearest and dearest.

The musician places himself in a suitable spot: on a low wall surrounding the well in the centre, so that he can be easily seen and heard. Is it too much to hope that he will take an accidental step backwards and disappear for good into the depths of that steep shaft?

He produces an empty leather scoop and places it on the wall beside him; then, with hands clad in specially knitted gloves that leave his fingertips exposed, strikes one single chord on the lute to stop all attempts at conversation.

"So, good folks of London," he begins, "what make you of the latest news from court?"

He gives a leer so foxy, you'd expect a brush to stick out of his behind.

The crowd start chattering excitedly in response, but this of course was not what he expected. He waits impatiently for them to settle down again.

"Quite right!" he calls out. "It beggars belief. Did you ever hear anything like it?"

Again, there are responses well beyond what his rhetorical questions would have intended. He has to strum his lute repeatedly before he can make himself heard again.

"At least!" he bellows, "it makes for a good ballad."

A white puff of steam issues as he opens his mouth to croon:

"Lady Rochford, Lady Rochford, as wicked as can be:
She lured a foolish maiden to commit adultery.
The girl will have to pay for it by parting with her head.
But it was Lady Rochford who induced her to be bad."

As might be expected, he invites those present to join in the chorus, and they all roar cheerfully, with or without something resembling a tune:

"But it was Lady Rochford who induced her to be bad!"

This ballad can be sung freely, in a public space right in the middle of London, with no risk of repercussion or retribution. Lady Rochford is fair game. Reviling her will hurt or offend no one.

Only her son, whose blood has turned as cold as the icy air of this winter's day.

The crowd, by contrast, is warming in anticipation of the next verse. I, too, listen with bated breath, in case the singer has some new information to impart.

"The poor old King was trusting: he did not see or heed
The Lady and the maiden preparing for their deed:
A dalliance as treasonous as dastardly and bold
Between the foolish maiden and her cavalier of old."

And he repeats:

"Lady Rochford, Lady Rochford, as wicked as can be:
She lured a foolish maiden to commit adultery.
The girl will have to pay for it by parting with her head.
But it was Lady Rochford who induced her to be bad."

Smirking their assent, the crowd need no encouragement to bawl:

"But it was Lady Rochford who induced her to be bad."

Though I have little sympathy for the woman purported to be my mother, I was appalled to see her executed, accused of being an accessory to the young queen's adultery. In my view this was a typical attempt by King Henry to apportion blame to anyone but himself.

But the populace have seized on this salacious theory. Coins are dropping into the scoop, as the balladeer continues:

"And then the wicked Lady wished for details to behold.
'You're wanted in the queen's bed,' another man was told.
Then all while they were at it, she lingered by the door.
Sent visitors apacking, to give them time for more."

The piquant detail appeals to the crowd: foolish grins remain stamped on their faces while the lute-player concludes:

"Lady Rochford, Lady Rochford, as wicked as can be:
She lured a foolish maiden to commit adultery.
For that she'll be beheaded, although we've heard it said
It's not much of a loss, for she's already off her head."

A hearty laugh resounds around the square, and all voices join in:

No, it's not much of a loss, for she's already off her head."

The singer picks up his scoop, rattling with contributions. I am left with the question that never stopped haunting me: Was she mad?

The Tower of London

February 1542.

This place looks vaguely familiar: it has old-fashioned architecture suggestive of the Tower of London, but the room is void of the splendour normally adorning this royal dwelling. It is in fact not much of a room, more like a coop some ten-foot square with a low vaulted ceiling. The small barred window does not let in much air, making for a foul atmosphere. The only furniture is a straw pallet, a three-legged stool and a board laid across rough trestles.

And there, reclining on the pallet, is my mother, dressed in plain black damask, her feet bare on cold stone flags. She looks pale and drawn, her hair hangs limp and loose. But her face is drawn into an eerie beatific smile, highly incongruent with her situation.

She gives a start as the door opens, shoots to her feet showing a hint of apprehension, which however turns into pure astonishment, as she sees who her visitor is.

"Lady Mary!"

Her weird shrill voice cuts a swathe through the rank air.

"Or should I say, Mrs Stafford?"

She makes a mock bow. "

"This, I say, comes as a surprise. In my new straitened circumstances I don't do much entertaining."

She takes two large strides towards her sister-in-law, places her hands on her shoulders and pushes her down on to the three-legged stool.

"This is as much hospitality as I am able to offer. Be grateful at least that the latrine bucket has been emptied. That doesn't happen every day."

This with an extravagant gesture towards a wooden bucket pushed into a corner of the room.

Shifting uneasily on her stool, Mary keeps her eyes lowered.

"I had to see you for myself," she mumbles.

"So sweeet of you to take the trouble."

Jane does not sound remotely as if she means it.

231

Mary looks up at her.

"I met up with Jojo yesterday," she says. "He wanted to come with me here today but I said I'd check with you first."

At the mere mention of my name Jane wrinkles up her nose as if it brought a smell even worse than the latrine bucket in the corner.

"I don't want to see him!"

"Your son has grown up into a fine young man," Mary goes on, suddenly animated. "A scholar of divinity, no less. He offered to help prepare you for what is to come."

"Keep that little rat away from me!" my mother snaps.

Mary looks at her sadly.

"You really are mad."

"Ha ha," laughs Jane, "that's what they all think. Just because I'm highly amused."

"I did hope," Mary says sincerely, "that would be the case."

Jane's eyebrows shoot up in query.

"It will make it easier for me to forgive you."

"Well I'm sorry to disappoint you," her sister-in-law sneers, "but I've never been more sane."

As she throws herself down again on the pallet, Mary asks her in a gentle voice, the way you would approach a lunatic, if she is aware that she is about to lose her head.

"Indeed," Jane replies. "But that's a small price to pay. Who needs a head when you've got what you've spent your life hankering after?"

"What would that be?"

"Revenge!" she cries triumphantly.

And then she starts laughing. She laughs so much it is a good while before she can go on speaking.

"They say the King – that putrid mountain of lard – has been weeping incessantly for weeks. It seems he really loved – or put it into his head that he loved – that silly slip of a girl."

She starts laughing again:

"He's devastated!"

More laughter. Tears are running down her cheeks.

"Oh Jane," is all Mary, deeply distressed, can come up with.

The laughter stops as suddenly as it started.

"And you," Jane says coldly, "I see, are as smug as ever. Not that you have anything to be smug about. But that was always the case with you."

Mary is unperturbed.

"I have everything I could possibly wish for."

"You have nothing!" Jane spits at her. "A simple commoner for a husband and hardly enough to eat."

Mary's gaze, as she contemplates her sister-in-law, betrays only pity.

"You have never known love, have you?"

"I've known what's much sweeter," Jane hisses. "Hatred!"

"That's a venom lethal also to yourself."

"Your love," snorts Jane, "will be buried with you. But my hatred will live on. The effect of it will never be forgotten."

To that, Mary has no reply to offer.

"You loved that oaf, Henry," her sister-in-law goes on, "not realizing that he was only using you. Like Francis and his filthy courtiers. Like men have been using women since time immemorial."

"The King in my day was an easy man to love."

A tender look flickers through Mary's eyes at the memory of the man she once knew – a man who exists no longer.

Jane has different ideas.

"Henry throughout his life has been driven by one pitiful force only: his male vanity. But that's been stifled now. That's why he can't stop bawling. I've revealed to all and sundry just what his virility is worth."

And she starts laughing again.

"I warrant it will never again rear its ugly head!"

Mary looks at her, concerned.

"Why do you hate him so?".

The answer is instant and emphatic:

"He destroyed my life."

All of a sudden, I notice that my father has appeared in the shadows. Though keeping his distance, he is, like me, riveted to the scene taking place before him.

His wife, my mother, meanwhile has taken to her feet, to pace restlessly on and off, like a caged animal. As she stops at the far end of the coop, she seems to have undergone another violent change of mood, for she addresses her sister-in-law in an almost normal conversational tone:

"Have you heard the ballad going around about me?"

"I've been told about it."

"So now all three of us are immortalized in song," Jane states dispassionately. "The whore, the witch and the bitch. That's how we'll go down in history."

Mary's response is, she cares little about history.

"I am happy with things as they are."

Jane scoffs.

"An impoverished commoner?"

At this point my aunt comes clean. She tells her sister-in-law that she is far from impoverished, having inherited Grandma Butler's fortune.

Jane seems dismayed by this news, then seizes on the one thing Mary can't do anything to alter:

"You're still plain Mrs Stafford."

But Mary smiles.

"Plain *beloved* Mrs Stafford."

I see a chink appear in my mother's offensive armour. What may have caused it? Envy at Mary's calm contentment? The discovery that her sister-in-law has in fact come out a winner? Her gaze wanders aimlessly around the room: pensive, dispirited and curiously bereft.

For some time she remains silent, brooding as it were, deliberating. Mary says nothing, just waits patiently for her sister-in-law to speak again.

"They've got it wrong, Mary," Jane says finally, in a tone that has changed once more — she sounds rational, not in the least insane. "They are all wrong about us."

"I know. But what can we do about it?"

"We can put the record straight."

Her voice is clear and calm.

Mary looks doubtful, knowing as she does that women have little hope of swaying a world of male power.

Jane is looking past her, into the distance.

"They made me vow never to tell anyone," she muses. "But now... What do I have to lose?"

Forgetting about Mary, I glance towards my father. He has withdrawn further into the darkness, though I can sense he is still there — tense, and watching intently.

"I think the time has come to speak up."

Jane turns to her sister-in-law and goes on, in a steady, deliberate voice:

"Yes, Mary, I will give it to you to pass on. Let the world know what happens to a pure and innocent young girl at King Henry's splendiferous court."

"What, Jane?" Mary inquires. "What could have happened to turn you into what you are? How does anyone become so vicious?"

In the pause that follows on this utterance, I see that both my grandmother and Anne have appeared in between my father and me. So now there are four of us keenly observing these long bygone proceedings.

Jane starts talking tonelessly into the room, addressing, as it were, no one in particular:

"On one occasion, while I was serving as maid of honour to Queen Catherine, my father fell very ill with fever. Dr Butt promised to watch over him at night, as I had to attend the queen. But I couldn't sleep for worry. I loved my father dearly. So in the dead of night I slipped away from the queen's apartment.

"In the long dark corridor leading to my father's quarters, I came across a group of young men returning after a night's revelling, wild roaring drunk. When they discovered me in the shadows, they mistook me for a servant-girl – I only had a shawl wrapped over my night shift.

"My presence met with hoots and laughter. One of them grabbed me from behind and shouted to the others that this was just what they needed."

She falls silent, taking a moment to collect herself.

"What did they do to you?" Mary asks softly.

"They took turns raping me. All five of them, egged on by their leader – even the little lute-player, though he protested at first that he was only there to provide the music."

Once more she pauses, as it were to gather the strength to continue.

"As a virgin, I hardly knew what was happening to me. All I was aware of was fear, and pain, and shame. When, finally, I was set free and staggered into my father's rooms, I was met by a shocked Dr Butts. He understood better than I did what had befallen me, and he tended to me as best he could. He said, with my father so ill, we had to protect him from any knowledge of the night's events. The mere thought might be enough to tip the scales of his recovery.

"In the weeks that followed, I identified, one by one, my assailants. I saw them going about the court as favoured attendants of the King. My father's health improved though he remained frail, and I said nothing about my ordeal. But then I had to go back to Dr Butts. I had started vomiting in the mornings. Dr Butt then talked to my father, and together they went to see the king."

"What was his reaction?"

"He was deeply embarrassed on behalf of his minions. My father and His Majesty had had the same strict moral code drummed into them by the king's devout grandmother. His Majesty lost no time promising he would mete out a suitable punishment for the miscreants and see to it that my future wasn't jeopardized."

My mother's face has resumed the bitter, pinched expression that I got used to seeing as a token of her habitual frame of mind.

Mary has to prompt her to continue.

"Were they punished?"

Jane heaves a deep sigh.

"Henry came up with what he termed a highly satisfactory solution. Granting me a generous stipend out of the royal coffers, he decreed that the leader of the rapists was to marry me and bring up the bastard as his own child. My reputation and my father's honour would thus be protected and the main culprit made to atone.

"The king was pleased, even amused by his ingenuity. Little did he care that I ended up the one most severely punished: chained for life to a man who resented my very existence. Who never came near me again."

Reluctantly, Mary is putting two and two together:

"Are you saying it was our George?"

"Yes. It was your George. Who had secretly touched my heart as a young page boy."

Mary state that her brother could never have done such a thing. He knew that Jane was Lord Morley's daughter. He wouldn't have dared touch her.

"They had me over a chest, Mary. Face down, taking me from behind. To them I was not a person, not a human being, not even a piece of flesh. All I was to them was... an orifice."

There is a long silence. I glance discreetly towards my father but can't see him in the darkness.

At length Mary speaks:

"Young Jojo — is this why you have always rejected him?"

"Well no one could expect me to embrace him with anything like affection."

"He couldn't help it!" Mary cries.

"Nor could I!" Jane cries back.

Another silence, this time broken by my mother.

"For years and years I suffered in silence, lonely and isolated, an unwanted member of your illustrious family, while my attackers rose higher and higher in power, wealth and position."

"Who were they? Apart from George?"

Jane rattles off the answer:

"Henry Norris, Francis Weston, William Brereton and Mark Smeaton."

Mary stares at her, as shocked as I am at the mention of these names.

"All of whom were executed for Anne's alleged adultery!"

Jane allows herself a smirk.

"You can't blame me for seizing a god-sent opportunity to administer my own justice."

"How did you manage it?"

"It was served to me on a silver salver. Cromwell had given me the task of spying on his behalf. Henry wanted Anne out of the way: I was to keep an eye out for anything that could incriminate her."

"I knew Cromwell was behind it!" mutters Mary.

"All I had to do was fabricate some evidence. Mark Smeaton helped by confessing."

"On the rack!"

"Whatever."

"But how," says Mary, "could you do this to Anne? She had never done anything to hurt you."

Jane replies that she did reckon that her haughty sister-in-law would be in trouble, that it wouldn't be such a bad thing to get her off her high horse.

"But I swear to God, Mary – I never thought Henry would kill her. His own wife, whom he had loved and cherished for so long. The mother of his child… Who would have thought he'd go that far?"

"She died thanks to you!"

"It wasn't my intention!"

"And the others?"

"They," says Jane simply, "got what they deserved."

Another silence. Mary stares, dumbstruck, at the floor.

"So you see, dear sister-in-law," Jane concludes, "I'm not mad at all. I'm glad I told you my story and I rely on you to ensure that everyone gets to know it."

"Me?"

"Yes, you Mary. Shout it from the rooftops when I'm dead and gone. Give me a chance to rest in peace."

Mary gets up from her stool, to stand very still, her back to her sister-in-law.

"Jane – " she says at length. "I can't do that."

"I'm requesting it of you. As my dying wish."

"Imagine what that knowledge would do to your son."

"I don't care about him."

"But I do," says Mary, turning round to face her. "Someone has to."

Jane seems ready to launch an objection, but she is cut short.

"I'm sorry, Jane. That's my last word."

Mary makes for the door. Before closing it behind her, she glances back at Jane over her shoulder.

"I'm glad to see you've stopped laughing."

The Sphere of Light

Here, in the sphere of light, they have all gathered around me: Anne and Elizabeth to one side, Mary and Jane to the other. And, lurking on the periphery, an unfamiliar representation of the man I once took to be my father: rueful and contrite, bereft of his former courtly swagger.

"So now I know," I address them all, making no effort to hide the sour bitterness in my voice. "What was always kept from me."

Seeing them look away, as well they might, I am seized by a violent rage, such as I have never felt before: its main target the ignoble figure half-in, half-out of the light.

"You!" I spit out. "You were the cause of it all!"

And I add with biting sarcasm:

"Thank you very much – 'father'!"

The man in question looks even more crushed.

"A moment's madness," he mumbles, "that could never be undone."

Loathing rises inside me like bile. Unable to bear the sight of him, I turn instead on the person closest to me on my left. Seeing her flinch only serves to fuel my anger.

"And you, Mary, knew and said nothing! You let me go through life thinking I was something other than the rotten fruit of a multiple rape! A bastard sired by one of five drunken revellers!"

"All I wanted," she defends herself tremulously, "was to protect you."

"I had to die!" I roar, "to discover the truth about myself!"

"Because the truth would have been too painful to live with."

The glint of a tear in her eye momentarily disarms me but does little to assuage my wrath, which now seeks out the two women of my right: Anne and Elizabeth.

"And you two!" I say accusingly. "What did you do to help? Other than stand idly by, as you're doing now? Turning a blind eye, for the sake of convenience!"

They both assure me that they knew nothing, they had no idea. Anne reminds me that she had to pay for it with her head, and my grandmother sadly recalls that she lost her will to live.

This exchange being less than satisfactory, I have only one person left on whom to vent my ire: my mother, who is looking increasingly discomfited – I would even say vulnerable, which must be a first for her.

"And you!" I growl. "You had no right to take it out on me! An innocent child, who had done nothing to deserve your hatred! I was entitled to my mother's love! All my life I pined for it!"

My attack is countered meekly:

"I had no love to give, Jojo. My heart had been forfeited. There were times when I reached for it... but it wasn't there."

We all look at her.

"A heartless person," Jane continues, "has no concept of right or wrong."

I'm moved by the sadness in her voice, the infinite sadness that comes with admission of guilt.

And it seems I'm not the only one to be affected. Her husband, Lord Rochford, has taken a step into the bright circle. My eyes are drawn to him: he is standing stock still, his gaze set upon my mother, taking her in, as it were, for the first time. Something is happening to him, I can see it in his eyes, they reflect some overwhelming sentiment or, rather, a compound of sentiments: on the one hand, shame, regret, remorse... on the other, concern, sympathy and – dare I say it? – tenderness?

"Jane..." he breathes, as if he can't trust his voice to carry.

She gives him a look, first full of doubt, then of astonishment, as he steps closer and goes down before her on one knee, burying his face in his hands.

Having seemed initially confounded by the supplicant at her feet, my mother, too, undergoes a change. Her features soften, the ingrained mask of acrimony falls away. Something in her stance suggests benevolence. Dear God, I say to myself. Dead though she is, her heart at long last is coming alive!

She holds out her arms tentatively towards her husband, but with his face still sunk into his palms, he does not notice. So she takes his hands and pulls him to his feet to stand facing her.

Their eyes meet and hold.

The rest of us watch dumbfounded, until my grandmother breaks the silence:

"And they say there's no beauty in death."

In the pause that follows, I search for an excuse to rekindle the fury that I felt clamoured for a release. All of those present have done their best to defuse it, but now I'm reminded that one person remains who has an awful lot to answer for.

"Where is King Henry?" I ask peremptorily. "Why is there no sign of him?"

"Poor Henry," Mary sighs, still able to think kindly of the man who treated her so badly. "He's still skulking in the tunnel."

"Accompanied, I imagine," Elizabeth adds, "by my husband. Who could never see beyond life at court."

"They both abhor the light."

This from Anne.

Lord Rochford admits that he himself had quite a struggle leaving the tunnel.

Then he turns back to his wife.

"I'm glad I made it out eventually."

"So am I," she says.

And their eyes lock once more.

Another pause, and then, with a sweeping glance, Elizabeth gathers us all up like a mother hen:

"Well, my dears. I'd say time has come for us to move on."

"Yes," Anne agrees. "We're free to go now. Thanks to Jojo. He's helped release us."

I have no idea what she means.

"By asking the right questions," Mary explains. "Questions the rest of us shirked."

"And now we have all the answers," my grandmother goes on, "there is nothing to keep us here."

"But –" I protest. "One important question remains!"

They look at me inquiringly.

"Who am I?

This meets with bewilderment.

"On the basis of likelihood," I begin reasonably, "I don't have a drop of Boleyn blood."

They all burst out laughing.

"Blood, he said!" That's my mother.

Anne gives me a nudge.

"There's no blood here, silly."

"You're still my Jojo," Mary assures me.

"And mine!" Anne endorses.

"And mine!" echoes my grandmother.

"And ours!" comes jointly from my parents, who are still standing close together, holding hands.

My parents? Have I reverted to thinking of Lord Rochford as my father?

"Will you come with us?" Mary asks. "Into the great unknown?"

"To whatever awaits us there," Anne fills in.

"Maybe nothing at all," warns Elizabeth.

"It could be the end of us," Jane muses.

Lord Rochford turns to his wife. "Are you afraid?" he asks softly.

She smiles at him, her eyes shining like beacons. "No. Are you?"

"Not in the least," he replies.

And with that the two of them, still hand in hand, leave the sphere of light.

Mary sends a glance after them.

"It's what we come here for," she states. "To discover what matters."

"And what does not," Anne concludes.

"The truth," I hear myself saying.

My grandmother inclines her head benignly.

"That is the beauty of death."

She offers her arm to Anne, who happily links up with hers and so they, too, depart for the darkness of the great unknown.

I gaze at the empty space they leave behind, suddenly wistful. Then I feel the light touch of a hand on my arm: My Aunt Mary. Sweet, gentle Mary, who taught me what love is all about.

"Jojo," she says softly, "what are you thinking?"

"I'm wondering whether I shall see Beatrice again. Will she be there, waiting?"

Mary smiles tenderly.

"If she is, my William will be there with her."

She slips her slender arm around my waist and I wrap my arm around her shoulder.

For a moment we stay like that, drawing strength from each other.

And then we're off.

Author's notes

My first close look at the Boleyn story raised more questions than answers: royal affection bestowed and withdrawn at random? A purportedly lecherous king – spending seven years in celibacy – before he breaks with Rome and makes England Protestant – all to make Anne Boleyn his wife – only to have her beheaded three years later when his lust takes another fancy – on trumped-up charges, along with five of his own associates,? And then another Boleyn lady – putting her head on the line and indeed losing it – for no apparent reason?

Decades of continued study revealed that factors such as contradictory evidence, malicious slander, and political intrigue had all conspired to obscure the truth of what really happened. Simplistic explanations like megalomania, sexual obsession, even insanity, have survived into our day.

As for Anne Boleyn – she is often portrayed as an ambitious young lady, pushed by her greedy, sycophantic family into the arms of a libidinous king, in a determined effort to get her to the throne of England. The myth has subsisted for close to five hundred years, appearing time and again, in novels and TV series, even in accounts claiming to be historically correct. In reality, this chapter of English history was driven by forces far beyond England's shores, far beyond royal passion, and far beyond any aspirations of the Boleyns.

At this time, England was in a politically feeble position, at risk of invasion by either of the two great European powers: France and the Holy Roman Empire, which included Spain, and in abject need of alliance with one of them as a shield against the other. In addition, civic unrest loomed at home. The Tudor claim to the throne was by many considered spurious, acquired as it was by violence, inherited only through the female line.

What England needed at this time was a strong, confident monarch. Henry VIII was neither. For one thing, he was never meant to be king. After the unexpected death of his elder brother Arthur, groomed for the crown, King Henry VII lamented publicly that his younger son did not have the qualities required of a king. Subjecting his offspring to such a judgement is the worst thing a parent can do. Henry never got over it, for the rest of his life he remained insecure, and most of his reign was spent in actions to disprove his father. With a weak ego that needed constant boosting, he did not take kindly to being challenged. Royal power was quickly applied to stamp out any opposition, becoming increasingly ruthless as resistance to the crown mounted.

Once he had succeeded as king of England at the age of seventeen, Henry was keen to foster an image of himself as an ideal Renaissance prince He excelled at courtly pursuits: hunting and jousting, dancing and singing, and surrounded himself with courtiers who were elegant, clever and accomplished – such as Thomas Boleyn and his son George. The king affectionately referred to the pleasure-seeking young courtiers as his 'minions'. But when their wild behaviour got out of hand, they were quickly expelled. Henry did not tolerate immorality at his court.

Henry' looked upon King Francis I of France as his arch rival. Impressing him was the whole reason for the mad extravagance of the Field of the Cloth of Gold in 1520, an exercise costing English taxpayers a fortune! No effort was spared to give a great impression: a temporary palace was erected, covering some two and a half acres. Walls were up to ten feet high, with huge expanses of glass, a profusion of golden ornaments, carved and painted decorations, and red wine flowing from fountains. Over five thousand royal attendants had been brought over from England, and nearly three thousand horses. In addition, some two thousand eight hundred tents were added for less distinguished visitors.

Tournaments, banquets and masques were presented, but the attempts to dazzle the King of France with all these entertainments had little effect. The highly sophisticated and grossly licentious Francis looked upon Henry as a naive upstart from a culturally inferior country.

And a wrestling match between the two monarchs turned sour when Henry lost.

Contrary to a common view, King Henry VIII was not lascivious. He had been strictly brought up by his deeply religious grandmother Margaret Beaufort, prepared by her for priesthood and a life of chastity. He remained prudish and impressed with purity. There is no evidence that he was anything but faithful to his first wife, Catherine of Aragon, for a number of years – as long as she could support his favoured persona as a romantic, chivalrous knight.

Henry's first acknowledged extramarital affair was with one of the queen's maids of honour, Bessie Blount. It may have started around 1515 and ended in 1519, after she bore him a son. The king gave the boy land and a dukedom. He was proud to be seen having fathered a son – he reckoned it proved that the failure in producing a male heir lay with Queen Catherine, not with him. There was even talk of this young man succeeding him, if all else failed. However, he died of consumption in 1536.

The king was still attractive, physically in his prime, when his eye fell on Mary Boleyn. Married to a member of the king's inner circle, she was conveniently at hand. During the years their liaison lasted, Henry handed out generous royal favours for her and her family. And he made no secret of the fact that he was deeply attached to Mary.

Only one portrait of Mary is known to exist. Many copies of this portrait have been made. It refers to Mary as 'Mary Bullen'. A common theory is that 'Bullen' was the family's original English name, and that it was amended, along with the family's social advancement, to the more sophisticated, frenchified 'Boleyn'. Another theory suggests the opposite, that the family was originally French, or perhaps Norman, stemming from the town of Boulogne, or Boleyne, as it was formerly called. So Boleyn may have been their original name that was later anglicised to Bullen. This theory is supported by the fact that the name written on the portrait is from a later than date the painting itself. Interestingly, Thomas Boleyn's grave here at Hever, in St. Peter's Church, names him as Thomas Bullen. Perhaps the Boleyn name had connotations that had become simply too notorious.

Mary Boleyn became conspicuously absent from early 1526. The prevalent reason is that "Henry got tired of her, fancied a change." But why was she disgraced? She did not show her face at court again until Anne was queen, and when her husband died, she did not get her rightful window's pension. Even her father wouldn't help her out. What had she done to deserve it?

Mary gave birth to two children while married to a courtier named William Carey: a daughter named Katherine, born around 1523, and a son called Henry, born in February 1526. There is doubt about the paternity of both children, but Henry is generally assumed to have been the king's son. He was never officially recognised like Bessie Blount's son, but even so, the boy was taken at a very young age from Mary. As a ward of his aunt Anne Boleyn, he was brought up by Cistercian monks at Syon Abbey and then educated at Hunsdon Manor along with his first cousin and, probably, half-sister Princess Elizabeth.

So what was the reason for Mary's apparent downfall? The timing of it coincides with the so-called Eltham Ordinances, a cost-cutting exercise by the Lord Chancellor, Cardinal Wolsey, and a golden opportunity for him to rid the court of officials he considered a threat to his own authority. The high-ranking Boleyns topped the list – but their positions were secure as long as Mary was in favour.

Help to discredit Mary seems to have been granted by the French king, who may have known Mary during her early days at the Paris court. He is on record as referring to Mary Boleyn as "a very great whore, the most infamous of them all". This may have been a ruse by the snide Francis I to bait Henry, who measured himself almost obsessively against his French counterpart. Highly sensitive where his manhood was concerned, not to mention his male honour, King Henry would have found it hard to stomach boasts by his arch rival about sex with the lady known to have won his own heart.

Blaming the woman was one way of protecting diplomatic relations: Mary ended up disgraced.

It has to be remembered that Mary was very young, in her early teens, when she and her sister Anne arrived at the French court in 1514. They came as maids of honour to Princess Mary Tudor, who was to marry King Louis XIII, some thirty years older than herself. The king died less than three months after the wedding, purportedly having overexerted himself in the marriage bedchamber. Mary Tudor returned to England after remarrying her husband of choice, the Duke of Suffolk.

The Boleyn girls stayed in France, Anne as a member of the pious Queen Claude's household at Blois, while Mary stayed at court in Paris. If she was ordered into Francis's bed and then passed round his courtiers, as has been alleged – who was she to refuse?

What records suggest is that rumours of Mary's loose behaviour at the French court reached her father in England and that he travelled to Paris in 1520 to bring her back to England, where she was married off to William Carey, an inveterate courtier.

With Mary gone from his life, how come Henry settled straight away for her sister Anne? Perhaps as a replacement for Mary, someone like her but with a stainless reputation and a better education. A gifted child, Anne had been chosen ahead of her older sister to join Margaret of Austria's court in Mechelen and subsequently became close to Queen Claude of France. With a French war looming, Anne was brought back to England in ·

1522. She arrived at the court: stylish, cultured and sophisticated and, above all, with a high price on her virtue.

A husband had been lined up for her: James Butler of Kilkenny. The marriage was intended to solve a dispute over the Boleyns' Irish heritage. However, Anne refused to be part of the scheme. She had her aims set on a good marriage with a man of her own choosing. And she remained impervious to the king's early overtures, determined not to follow in the footsteps of her by now discarded sister. Henry had to hold out the prospect of a crown to sway her, and even then, she would not come to his bed until their wedding was imminent.

Henry was prepared to wait. His prime concern was not to have a sexy new mistress, but a male heir! With England's position so precarious, Henry depended on support from France, especially since any attempt to divorce Catherine of Aragon would seriously antagonise the powerful emperor Charles V, who was Catherine's nephew.

With a talent for massaging facts to suit his aims, King Henry managed to fabricate an excuse on religious grounds to declare his marriage to Catherine of Aragon invalid. She had been married to his brother and according to the Bible, Leviticus 20-21. this made the union "blighted in the eyes of God". That, Henry concluded, was the reason why the marriage had failed to produce the necessary male heir! Convinced of the righteousness in his reasoning, Henry fully expected the pope to grant an annulment.

But Pope Clement VII was wary of aggravating the powerful Emperor Charles V, Queen Catherine's nephew. And following the brutal sacking of Rome by imperial troops in 1527, leaving the pope the emperor's prisoner, there was no question of Pope Clement moving on an annulment for the English king. On the other hand, he had no wish to create a rift, in case England's support was needed in future. So he did pretend to help by sending his legate Cardinal Campeggio to London for a trial. After endless procrastination, it eventually took place at Blackfriars in

1529. It ended, as fully intended, inconclusively. Pope Clement was determined to remain on the fence – indefinitely, up until his death in 1534.

What was generally referred to as "the English king's great matter" became part of an ongoing battle for supremacy on the European continent. With no hope of support for divorce coming from Spain, Henry depended heavily on France as his ally. Years passed, as Henry pursued ways and means to achieve the royal divorce: first on religious grounds, then legally, after that academically, and above all, politically. His determination to marry Anne Boleyn was not due to blind affection or untrammelled lust, but to a dogged refusal to be thwarted by his political enemies. Their romance remained unconsummated.

While the king was above reproach, Anne faced much criticism. Most English women supported Queen Catherine, seeing Anne as a threat to the sanctity of marriage, on which they all depended. Denigrating reports by the emperor's ambassador Eustace Chapuys, referring to her only as "the concubine", were designed to humour Emperor Charles V. Depictions by Anne's many enemies have tainted her character ever since.

Throughout, the alliance with France remained absolutely essential. In 1532, Henry took Anne to Calais, still an English possession, where Francis was royally entertained to ensure his support did not wane. But then, to his dismay, it transpired that Francis had recently entered an alliance with Pope Clement, arranging for his son Prince Henri (later Henri IV of France) to marry Catherine de Medici –the pope's niece! It is at this time that Henry decides to break with Rome – a highly relevant co-incidence. I have never seen it referred to anywhere, but it explains why and when Henry gave up on political manoeuvring and simply took the law into his own hands, divorced Catherine of Aragon and married Anne Boleyn.

As expected, relations with Emperor Charles V deteriorated further after Henry's marriage to Anne, but imperial diplomacy was maintained by blame being imperially apportioned to Anne and her family.

In May 1533, the pregnant Anne was crown Queen of England in a ceremony as extravagant as the crowning of a king. But in September, the birth of Princess Elizabeth was a huge disappointment for the king, who had been counting on a son. Much as he expected a son to follow, all that Anne achieved in the few years that followed was miscarriages.

With Cardinal Wolsey dead and gone, Henry's first minister, the ruthless Thomas Cromwell, took the view that a new alliance with the Charles V was imperative, not only to avert the threat of a Spanish invasion but also for support against new hostile moves by France. But there was no chance of a treaty with Spain as long as Anne was Queen of England. She had to go – had to be eliminated, drastically and definitely, by execution.

There was only one problem. If Anne was removed from the throne, there would be pressure from the emperor to reinstate Catherine, who was lingering, banished at Kimbolton Castle. However, in early January 1536, Catherine died, instantly removing Anne's only safeguard.

Cromwell did his best to persuade the king, reminding him that Anne had failed in her main duty: to produce a male heir. When Henry was thrown from his horse during a tournament and gravely injured and Anne shortly afterwards gave birth to a stillborn son, the necessity of changing to another, fecund wife was intensified. Again, this was not a case of King Henry "being tired of one woman and fancying another". It was about the survival of England as nation.

So how to get rid of Anne and the rest of the Boleyn family?

What is not generally noted is that Cromwell was close to Lord Morley, who was the father of Jane Boleyn, now Lady Rochford, wife of Anne's brother George. Lady Rochford was a member of Anne's inner circle! It is highly likely that she was approached through her father and instructed to find evidence to discredit Anne.

Jane willingly obliged, giving evidence that helped to have not only her sister-in-law Anne executed, but also her own husband George and four of the king's close associates. But why did she do this? What could have been her reason?

Let's go back to another question: What drove George Boleyn to marry Jane Parker when he was barely out of his teens? She was the daughter of a minor, impoverished aristocrat, with no status worth mentioning, no inheritance beckoning. The Boleyn men were normally ambitious in their choice of wife, marrying well above their station: George's paternal grandmother was the daughter and heiress of the wealthy Earl of Ormond and his mother a daughter of England's premier duke, The Duke of Norfolk!

It has never been explained why King Henry gave Jane Parker a generous dowry out of the royal coffers, as well as donating a mansion, Grimston Manor in Norfolk, as a wedding present to the young couple?

No records are known of Jane and George Boleyn ever appearing together as a married couple – except for one occasion when both were present at the christening of Jane's sister's child. This has been mooted as proof that their marriage was valid and working. However, George had his own reason to be present – the father of the child being christened was actually his own first cousin.

More poignantly, why is there no record of the Dean of Lichfield, also called George Boleyn, being born or present as a child? George and Jane are considered to have been childless. The Dean of Lichfield, in spite of his name, is dismissed by historians as "some distant relation" or possibly an illegitimate son of George Boleyn. But then he wouldn't have had his name.

There is also proof of a close link between Mary's son Lord Hunsdon and the Dean of Lichfield: The latter is named as the executor of Hunsdon's will – hardly a task you assign to some peripheral figure.

A lecturer in archeology at Galway University, hearing about my interest in the Boleyn family, alerted me to a 17th century tombstone at Colony Castle in Co. Offaly, Ireland. I went to see it, still in the grounds of the castle, and though the inscription is by now faded, it had been deciphered by the university and read as follows:

"HERE UNDER LEYS ELISABETH AND MARY BULLYN DAUGHTERS OF THOMAS BULLYN SON OF GEORGE BULLYN THE SON OF GEORGE BULLYN VISCOUNT ROCHFORD SON OF SIR THOMAS BULLYN ERLE OF ORMOND AND WILLSHEERE"

There are extant records of the two Boleyn sisters living at Colony Castle at this time. They are said to have had a pact that, when one of them died, the other one would throw herself to her death from the top of the keep, which seems to be what actually happened. There is also a record of a third Boleyn sister named Anne, who married a local farmer. Assuming that the tombstone is authentic, it is interesting to note that George Boleyn's grandson named his daughters after his female forebears – but excluded his grandmother Jane.

And this brings us to my personal theory that provides the answers to numerous questions. Author George Cavendish, best known for his biography of Cardinal Wolsey, accused Anne's brother George of "forcing widows and deflowering virgins". This may well have been true of his younger days, when the royal 'minions' took such liberties that they were banished from court until they agreed to mend their ways. My theory is that Jane was raped by George and possibly also by the other courtiers she falsely named as guilty of adultery with Anne.

If young Jane Parker was indeed one of the virgins forcibly deflowered by George and, as it looks, impregnated, her father Lord Morley would no doubt have filed a complaint with His Majesty. Having served in the household of Henry's grandmother, Lady Margaret Beaufort, Morley would have known Henry as a child and been well aware of the strict moral code that had been impressed upon him. The most likely response to an accusation of rape by one of his courtiers would have been for the king to order the guilty party, in this case George Boleyn, to marry his pregnant victim; this would serve to punish the perpetrator and, at the same time, safeguard the Morley family's honour.

The one who ended up the loser was Jane: chained for life to a husband who resented her; member of a family who held her in scant regard; and mother of a child she appears to have rejected.

After her husband's death, Jane Boleyn, Lady Rochford, was rewarded for her help in Anne's downfall with a position as chief lady-in-waiting to a succession of queens: first Jane Seymour, then Anne of Cleves. Lady Rochford was the one to spread the news that the marriage to Anne of Cleves remained unconsummated – a fact that the king quickly put down to, not his own impotence, but to the ugliness of his new wife – a myth that has persisted.

Lady Rochford is in fact a signatory to King Henry's divorce settlement with Anne of Cleves, jointly with another court lady, surprisingly my namesake – Ann Jocelyn. I have identified her on the Jocelyn family tree taking up a twelve-feet long wall in my home. Dr Damien Duffy has identified her as a lady-in-waiting close to Anne Boleyn as queen. It is the first sign of a link between the Boleyns and the Jocelyn family. They intermarried only in the late 18th century.

Jane's final appointment was as chief lady of the bedchamber to King Henry's fifth wife, the teenage Katheryn Howard, actually a first cousin of the Boleyn sisters. And this appointment became the end of her. Revealed as having induced the young queen to take in secret lovers, Jane was beheaded along with

Katheryn. So what could have driven her to do something so dangerous – and foolish? The usual answer is that she was mad – and perhaps she was.

It was plain to everyone at court that Henry was besotted with his young fifth wife. As a narcissist, he depended on others to confirm his worth and little Katheryn Howard, well groomed for pleasing older men, played along with him. Henry's manhood had suffered badly with Anne of Cleves, who was not ugly – just disgusted by the unhealthy, obese, smelly and revolting Henry. Unable to hide her disgust, she had rendered him impotent. Now, young Katheryn Howard made him feel a man again.

In spite of her royal favours, Lady Rochford may well have been possessed by obsessive hatred against the king, who had ruined her life by condemning her to a life of misery, whilst the perpetrators of her crime were let off scot free. And here was an irresistible opportunity to destroy him, even at the cost of her own head.

Both Boleyn parents, Thomas and Elizabeth, broken socially and probably emotionally, died within years of the execution of Anne and George. Elizabeth was so disenchanted with the Boleyn family, she chose to be buried in the Howard family chapel at Lambeth. Thomas Boleyn has his grave in St. Peter's church here at Hever.

The one survivor was Mary Boleyn, who had been banished from court for a second time after marrying a commoner, William Stafford, in 1534. She is quoted as saying that she would "rather beg her bread with him than be the greatest queen in Christendom".

Thomas Boleyn's mother, born Lady Margaret Butler, was the daughter of the prosperous Earl of Ormond. Unusually for a woman at the time, she had inherited one half of her father's considerable wealth. And when she died in 1539, shortly after her son Thomas, she left her fortune to Mary, who thus ended up having riches as well as love. Sadly not for long, as she died, possibly of plague, in 1543. Her wealth was divided between her husband William Stafford and her son Lord Hunsdon, enabling them both to establish themselves as members of Parliament.

During the violent reign of the Catholic Bloody Mary, Lord Hunsdon and his sister, now married as Catherine Knollys, managed to stay safe in England, in spite of being Protestant. Mary Boleyn's husband William Stafford took refuge in Geneva with his and Mary's two children. He died there in 1556. What happened to the children is not known. They may have died of the disease that took their father's life, or else they stayed on the continent, living in obscurity.

Mary Boleyn's Carey children both had very large families, and so her line survives to this day. Among her descendants, through the late Queen Mother, they include King Charles. Princess Diana also descended from Mary, so her genes are very much present in today's royal family.